Robin Jones Gunn

PUBLISHING

Colorado Springs, Colorado

ISLAND DREAMER

Copyright © 1992 by Robin Jones Gunn

Library of Congress Cataloging-in-Publication Data
Gunn, Robin Jones, 1955-
    Island Dreamer / Robin Jones Gunn.
        p. cm. -- (Christy Miller series)
    Summary: Christy Miller visits Hawaii, where she turns
sixteen and overcomes her fear of driving during an island adventure.
    ISBN 1-56179-072-9
    [1. Hawaii--Fiction.] I. Title. II Series: Gunn, Robin Jones,
1955- Christy Miller Series.
PZ7.G972Is 1992
[Fic} -- dc20

                                          92-3938
                                            CIP
                                            AC

Published by Focus on the Family Publishing, Colorado Springs,
Colorado 80995

Distributed in the U.S.A. and Canada by Word Books, Dallas, Texas.

Edited by Janet Kobobel
Designed by Sherry Nicolai Russell
Cover illustration by Phil Boatwright

Printed in the United States of America

92 93 94 95 96 97 / 10 9 8 7 6 5 4 3 2 1

To my kindred spirit, Donna Hendrix,
whose rich, fragrant friendship
over the years has opened up to me
the mystery of "God-things."

Contents

Acknowledgments   **vii**

1. What's So Funny?   **1**

2. Do You Want to Know a Secret?   **12**

3. If Only Katie Could Fit in My Suitcase   **31**

4. Flight 272 Is Now Boarding   **47**

5. Aloha!   **59**

6. "Sweet" Sixteen?   **76**

7. Come On, Christy, Show Us How to Hula!   **96**

8. Mystery Call From the Blue Grotto   **109**

9. Mosquito Nets and Prayers   **125**

10. Which Way to the Waterfalls?   **136**

11. The Bridge   **144**

12. Hana After It Rains   **151**

13. The "God-Thing"   **169**

Acknowledgments

I affectionately appreciate the contributions of Juliette Montague Cooke, who sailed from New England in the 1840s to be a missionary to the Hawaiians on the island of Oahu. Her diary, which I read while writing this book, changed my heart and how I told this story. I can't wait to meet her in heaven.

Mahalo to Mark, Claire, Joe, Maureen, Bud, Lola, Mark, Nancy and all our brothers and sisters at Kumulani Chapel, Lahaina, Maui, for your aloha and kokua at a time we needed it most.

Chapter 1

What's So Funny?

I'm really going to miss you, Todd. I hope you have a good time." Christy Miller flipped her nutmeg brown hair behind her ear and pressed the phone closer with her shoulder, waiting for his reply.

Todd laughed and said, "Hey, we're both going to have a good time."

Christy switched the phone to her other ear and crossed her long legs. "Yeah, I guess I'll have a good time with Paula when she gets here. But I wish I was going to Maui with you and Uncle Bob. How long do you think you'll be gone?"

"Two or three weeks," Todd answered in his easygoing manner. "Depends on how long it takes us to paint and do all the repairs on Bob's two condos. So, when does your friend get here?"

"Paula's coming tomorrow. If you stay in Maui longer than two weeks, you won't even get to meet her," Christy said, releasing a heavy sigh. "I guess I thought all along that you'd be here when she came, and we could go places together. Only now, you're going to Maui, and Paula and I will be stuck here in Escondido!"

1

Todd chuckled as if what Christy said amused him. "Like I said, we'll all have a good summer. You'll see."

He paused, and Christy wished just this once he would say something tender and meaningful like "I'll miss you" or "I wish you were coming." She fingered the gold ID bracelet he had given her and waited.

"Hey, I have to get my stuff together. Your uncle's going to be here in about twenty minutes."

"Okay, well, I know you'll have a great time." Christy switched from her moping tone to a teasing voice and said, "And I know better than to ask you to write me. But maybe you could send me one little postcard of a waterfall or something tropical to help me feel even more depressed that I'm not there with you."

He laughed again. For being such a wonderful heartthrob of a guy, Todd could also be a brat. What did he think was so funny?

"I'll see you, Chris. Aloha!" Click.

That's how abruptly he usually ended his phone conversations. As usual, Christy kept holding the receiver to her ear, hearing the dial tone and dreaming about what it would be like if Todd ever talked to her on the phone the way Rick did.

She considered Rick only a friend, yet when he called a few weeks ago to tell her about his upcoming trip to Europe, he had said things like "When I look into the blue Danube, I'll be remembering your blue-green killer eyes."

At the time, all Christy could think was *Oh, brother!* Yet, if Todd ever said something like that, she'd absolutely melt.

Placing the receiver back in its cradle, Christy hopped down from her perch on the kitchen counter and tugged open the refrigerator door in search of breakfast.

Mom walked through the kitchen, lugging a laundry basket bulging with dirty clothes. "Christy! I didn't realize you were up already."

"We're out of milk," Christy mumbled. "Mom, how come Dad works for a dairy, yet we're always running out of milk?"

"We had half a gallon in there last night. Your brother must have used it up this morning. Banana muffins are in the basket on the counter, and orange juice should be in the freezer."

Mom paused and rested the basket on the counter. "Oh, did you call Todd yet? He and Bob are leaving for Maui this morning, you know."

Christy peered over the top of the open refrigerator door at her round-faced mother, standing a few feet away. Christy heard suppressed laughter in Mom's voice, and one look at her big grin proved it. Her own mother thought there was something funny about Todd going away for several weeks.

It wasn't funny! Christy was going to miss him terribly, even though they lived too far away to see each other more than once a week during the summer.

"Yes, I called him." Her words came out chopped and her actions swift as she closed the refrigerator door.

"I just wondered," Mom said in a motherly way before stepping down into the garage to start the laundry.

"Oh, you're up." Christy's dad, a large man with reddish hair and strong hands, entered the kitchen and poured himself a cup of coffee. "Why don't you get dressed, and I'll take you driving?"

"Driving?"

"Yeah, driving."

"Today?" Christy felt as though someone had just put ice cubes down her back.

"We don't have to go," Dad said, opening the refrigerator and looking around, shuffling jars on the top shelf. "Where's the milk?"

"It's all gone," Christy answered, her thoughts still processing the paralyzing idea of driving today.

"We're out of milk?"

"I guess so. That's what Mom said."

Dad made a pinched face as he sipped his coffee black. "Come on, let's go driving. We can pick up some milk on the way back."

"Okay," she answered, doing an exceptional job of sounding as though she really wanted to go.

"Can you be ready in ten minutes?"

"Sure. I'll go get dressed."

"Margaret?" Dad called to Mom in the garage. "Why is it I work for a dairy, but we're always running out of milk?"

Why is it I really want my driver's license, but I'm always running out of courage to practice driving? Christy asked her reflection in the bathroom mirror. *Why do I freak out like this? I'm going to be sixteen in only . . .* She quickly counted. *. . .In five days. Five days! I've got to get over this fear, or I'll never get my license!*

Soaking a washcloth, she held it on her face and then bit

into the wet terry cloth, chomping down hard. *This is ridiculous! Everyone I know has a license. They all did it. What am I so afraid of?*

Twenty minutes later, sitting in the driver's seat of their parked car with Dad next to her, Christy knew exactly what she was afraid of. She was afraid of the car.

That was it. The power a car put at her command was scary. The possibility of misusing that power and getting hurt, or worse, hurting someone else—that's what she was afraid of.

"Dad," Christy began but then didn't know what to say.

"Ready?" Dad asked, cinching his seat belt and checking to make sure it was secure.

"Do you ever think about how fast, I mean, how a car could . . ."

Dad looked intently at her, his eyebrows pushed together, waiting for her to finish her thought.

"Never mind. I just feel a little nervous."

"Don't. If you let yourself get nervous, you'll be a nervous driver." Dad squared his shoulders and looked straight ahead. "Start the car, Christy."

She responded right away, swallowing her anxious thoughts and taking a quick peek at Dad out of the corner of her eye. How was she supposed to relax when her dad had braced his arm against the door and planted his feet on the floorboard, looking like he was about ready to take off in a rocket for Mars?

"Ten and two," Dad said.

"Ten and two?" Christy asked.

"Hands on the steering wheel at ten o'clock and two o'clock positions. Release the parking brake."

Christy followed his orders and tried to calm her heart, which had begun marching much faster than her brain.

"Okay. Put 'er in drive."

As soon as she slipped the gear shift to "D," Christy slowly pressed on the gas pedal. The car inched across the vacant church parking lot like a reluctant caterpillar. She made it to the other side of the lot without going more than seven miles per hour and promptly pushed on the brake. The car faced the back fence at a complete stop, and Christy glanced at her dad, awaiting his approval and further instructions.

He sat there with his chin tucked down to his chest and looked at her without turning his head. "That was very nice—if you plan to drive only through car washes the rest of your life."

Christy let out a loud bubble of laughter. Dad was right! It did seem as though they'd just driven through a car wash. As she laughed, she felt more relaxed.

Dad relaxed, too, and looked behind them. "Put 'er in reverse, and let's see you drive like you would on a city street."

Still smiling, Christy popped the gear to "R" and looked back over her right shoulder. She pushed the gas pedal, but nothing happened.

"Give 'er some gas," Dad said, still looking straight ahead.

So she did. She put her right foot down hard, and the car

lurched backward at a startling speed. Her hands jerked the wheel first to the right, then to the left.

Dad hollered, "Hit the brakes!"

So she did.

Bam! The bumper hit the cement base of a parking lot light pole, jerking their heads back, then forward.

"Put it in park. Turn off the engine," Dad barked and reached to turn off the ignition himself before ejecting from the passenger seat and running to the back of the car.

Christy sat completely still. Her lower jaw began to tremble, and she felt the hot tears bubbling up in her eyes. She didn't dare turn around. She couldn't move.

"Come here, Christy."

She blinked and forced her frozen arm to open the door and her wobbly legs to carry her to the back of the car. Dad pointed to the bumper.

"Could've been worse. I can pound it out. Best thing for you is to get right back in the saddle."

She couldn't believe Dad acted so calmly! She'd been sure the impact crushed the entire back end of the car. How could such a sickeningly huge thud cause so little damage?

Her face must have mirrored all her terrified feelings, because Dad slipped his arm around her shoulders and said, "Don't worry about it."

A few tears tumbled down her face. She pressed against Dad's chest and in a small, shaky voice said, "I'm really sorry. I just didn't . . . I mean, I was . . . I, I don't know."

From where her ear was pressed against Dad's chest, Christy heard a rumbling sound. She looked up at him, and he let out a roar of laughter. He kept laughing, and she smiled frantically, trying to figure out what was so funny.

"Look around," he invited.

She looked and saw nothing. No cars in the parking lot. No people. Only several parking lot lights planted strategically across the large lot.

"I don't see anything."

"Exactly," Dad said, smiling broadly. "What are the chances, in such a huge space, that you'd find something to run into?" He chuckled again.

For the third time that day, Christy felt a squeeze in her stomach, knowing she was the only one who didn't see what was so funny.

"I didn't mean to do it," she said defensively. "You said to give it gas."

"Now, Christy," Dad said, the laughter evaporating, "don't blame me and don't blame yourself either. That's why they're called accidents. Come on." He headed back to the passenger-side of the car. "Let's give it another try."

They went through the same seat-belting motions as before. Dad looked quite serious again. When Christy put the car in drive, she noticed Dad's right foot automatically hit the floorboard as if he were going for his invisible brakes.

Christy looked straight ahead and said, "Can I just ask you one little question?"

"Yes?" Dad faced forward, right arm braced against the door and left hand on his seat belt.

Christy playfully leaned forward, gripping the steering

wheel like a race car driver, and said with a giggle, "You sure your life insurance is paid up, Dad?"

"Now, don't get silly. Driving is serious business."

She could see the smile he suppressed and added in her best Disneyland ride-attendant voice, "Please keep hands and arms inside the moving vehicle at all times, and remember there is no flash photography."

Then smooth as can be she began her driving exercises around the parking lot.

"Let's hope there are no flashes of *any* kind," Dad said in a low voice. "Pay attention to what you're doing now. Turn right up here and go down to the end."

Greatly relieved and feeling more relaxed than before, Christy did what she considered to be a very good job of navigating the parking lot and told her mother so when they got home. She left out the part about the bumper, and thankfully, Dad was still outside so he couldn't fill in any of the missing details.

Christy flopped into the well-used recliner and hung her legs over the arm rest, waiting for Mom's encouraging comments.

"That's good, dear," Mom said, folding clothes and stacking them in neat piles on the couch. "Don't be disappointed, though, if you're not fully ready or able to get your license exactly on your birthday."

"I will be. Besides, it's a big deal here. I mean, maybe it wasn't back in Wisconsin when you were growing up, but everyone I know in California who is sixteen has a license.

I'd be embarrassed if I didn't."

Mom placed a folded T-shirt on Christy's pile of clean laundry and tossed her a mound of bath towels, still warm from the dryer, which Christy snuggled around her like a kitten in a feather bed.

"Those are for you to fold, not make a nest out of," Mom said. Then she added, "All I'm saying is you shouldn't try to take the test until you're completely ready."

Christy dropped the first folded towel to the floor beside the recliner. "Mom, do you think Uncle Bob really meant it when he said he'd pay for my insurance the first year?"

"Certainly. You do remember the condition, though. You must pass your test the first time you take it. He was very adamant about that. Which is why I'm saying, don't take the test until you're absolutely certain you'll pass. Oh, I almost forgot."

Mom handed Christy a letter that had been underneath the mound of laundry. "This came for you today."

Christy folded the last towel and took the letter from her mom. She didn't recognize the handwriting. The letter, written on a single piece of notebook paper read:

Dear Christy,

I've thought about what you said, and I think you're right. I'll tell you more about my decision when I see

That was all. The last sentence wasn't finished, and the letter wasn't signed.

"Who's this from?" Christy asked, scanning it again before trying to decipher the smeared postmark on the envelope.

Who wrote this? What did I say? And what kind of decision did somebody make based on something I said? This is strange!

Mom hadn't heard her. She stood by the screen door, a load of folded clothes in her arms, looking at Dad, who was bent over the back of the car in the driveway.

Christy decided to check the handwriting against some of Paula's old letters and started down the hall to her bedroom.

"Christy," Mom asked, "what is your father doing to the car? He has a hammer in his hand. Christy?"

Christy quickly slipped into her bedroom and quietly closed the door.

Chapter 2

Do You Want to Know a Secret?

This family sure doesn't know how to keep secrets," Christy complained to her mother the next morning in the car.

"Why do you say that?" Mom asked, changing into the fast lane on the freeway and glancing at her watch.

"When Aunt Marti called this morning, she knew all about what happened in the church parking lot yesterday."

"That's 'cuz I told her," David popped up from the backseat.

"Why?" Christy turned around and scolded her nine-year-old brother. "You don't have to always tell everybody everything."

David, a compact version of their dad, had a silly smile on his face. His funny look was exaggerated by his glasses sliding down his nose.

He ignored her by returning his attention to the miniature cars on the seat beside him. Rolling one of the cars along the vinyl seat, he spoke in tiny cartoon voices. "Look out! There's a telephone pole up ahead! Don't worry, it's over a mile away! Doesn't matter! Christy's driving! Oh, no! Aaaaayyee! Crash! Bang! Boom!"

Christy didn't do him the honor of turning around. She calmly said, "Mom, make him stop."

"David, don't make fun of your sister."

"I'm not, Mom. I saw this in a cartoon once. Really!"

"David!"

"Oh, all right. Can you put on a tape? When are we going to get there? Are we going to stop and get something to eat?"

"We've still got another hour before we get to the airport," Mom said, checking her watch again. "And no, we're not going to stop to get something to eat. You can wait until after we pick up Paula."

"Are we going to stay overnight at Aunt Marti's?" he asked.

"No, we'll probably just stay for lunch and then come home."

"How come I have to go to the airport with you? It's boring!"

"Because last night you begged to go," Mom answered. "Or did you forget?"

"I wish I'd stayed home." David folded his arms and leaned against the door.

"You're not the only one," Christy muttered under her breath.

"Christy!" Mom snapped. "Listen, you two, I want you both to try harder to be kind to each other, especially when we go . . ." She stopped, and they both waited for the rest of her scolding.

"Well, especially when we go places together like this.

Just try harder, all right?"

Neither of them answered, and Mom shot quick, serious glances at them. "All right?"

"Okay," came from the backseat.

"All right," Christy said with a sigh.

They did pretty well the rest of the drive into Los Angeles International Airport. The only disagreement they had came when Mom tried to hurry them to the gate where Paula's plane was about to land and David wanted to get a drink of water.

"Come on, David!" Christy yelled. "We don't have time!"

Mom had already scooted ahead of them into the flurry of people. As Christy took David by the arm, she could barely see which way Mom was going.

"Stay with me, David! It's too easy for a little kid like you to get lost in the mob."

He wiggled his arm free but stayed right by her side until they reached Mom, who was talking to somebody in the waiting area. Christy stepped up behind Mom. Since she was several inches taller than her mother, she could see over her shoulder, but she wasn't ready for what she saw.

"Paula?"

The Wisconsin farm girl with the baby-doll face and big, round, blue eyes jumped up and shrieked, colliding with David as she wrapped her arms around Christy in an exuberant hug.

"I'm here! I'm here!" she announced to Christy and everyone in the waiting area.

Paula looped her big bag-purse over her shoulder and breathlessly, dramatically said, "I was freaking out, you guys! I guess my plane came in early. About ten minutes early, they said. And I got off, and I didn't know anybody, and oh, man, I was really worried, and I just sat down and tried to be really calm and everything, and then your mom walked up, and I almost started crying, and then I saw you, and it was like it hit me that I was really here!"

Christy laughed at her friend's enthusiastic commentary. Paula had been like that ever since Christy could remember. She seemed "more" Paula than the Paula Christy grew up with and hadn't seen for almost a year.

"You cut your hair!" Christy exclaimed.

Paula fingered the side of her very short, stiffly moused hair and said, "I had to! You got yours cut when you came here last summer, and so I thought I should get the California look before I got here, but . . ."

Paula seemed to notice Christy for the first time. "You're growing yours out! I can't believe it's to your shoulders already! Last time I saw you it was short!"

Then her round cheeks turned a spicy shade of pink, and in a panic she said, "Oh, no! Is everybody growing their hair out this year? Am I the only one with short hair? Oh no!"

"Paula!" Christy laughed and spoke softly, hoping Paula would take the hint and lower her voice too. "You look great! This is California. You can wear your hair anyway you want. Don't worry! Relax!"

Mom suggested they pick up the luggage. As Paula chattered all the way through the terminal, Christy watched her and thought how really good Paula did look.

She always had been a little "cutie" with her long blond hair and innocent, little girl looks. Now, except for the same big, baby-doll eyes, Paula looked more like a young woman than a little girl. Her figure had turned out much better proportioned than Christy thought hers was, and the sophisticated hairstyle and obvious makeup made Paula look much older than her fifteen years.

It felt strange walking beside Paula, listening to her ramble on, oblivious to how loud she was and how people were turning to look at her. Christy thought of how the year they'd been apart had changed both of them and how she'd waited so long to see Paula again. Now that she was here, well, for some reason Christy felt squeamish.

"You know what I mean, Christy?" Paula said, snapping Christy back into the present.

"Oh, yeah. Uh huh." *Whatever you just said.*

"I mean, who knows when I'm going to get back here again, so while I'm here I want to see and do everything we can, and I've been saving up my money so you won't have to pay for me for anything, and maybe I can help pay for gas and stuff when we go places."

Mom calmly turned and spoke solid words to Paula, which made Christy listen carefully. "We will all have a good time, Paula. Just keep in mind you may get to see some things you didn't expect to see, and you may not get to see some things you hoped to."

"Oh, I know. My mom said the same thing. I'll be fine whatever we do, really. I don't want to be a bother or anything."

"You're not a bother," Mom said as they arrived at the crowded baggage claim. "We're glad you're here."

"Oh! Look! There are my bags already. That big plaid one and the two little ones next to it."

"Looks like you brought enough stuff to stay a month!" Christy teased as the girls stepped back and let Mom and David capture the moving targets.

"Oh, don't I wish! I had a hard enough time coming for two weeks, because we have this big family reunion I have to go to right when I get back. I'm going to have the best tan of anyone there too!"

Christy laughed at Paula's innocent comments. She sounded like such a playful little girl, yet everything in her blue eyes told Christy Paula had become very serious about her goals.

And she had a lot of goals!

The two girls shared the backseat during the hour and a half drive to Bob and Marti's. Paula went on about how her friend Melissa had gotten her a job at Dairy Queen and how she had saved all her money for the past seven months. She had more than two hundred dollars left, and that was after buying some new clothes and paying for half of her airfare.

"I have to buy a new bathing suit before we go to the beach. I'd just die if I had to wear my old one, and people started to laugh at me like they did at you last summer."

"They didn't really laugh at me," Christy defended.

"Yes they did. When you wrote me, you said they made fun of your green-bean bathing suit!"

"Is that right, Christy?" Mom asked, looking in the rearview mirror. "You never told me that."

It was one of those embarrassing moments Christy didn't want to repeat, especially to her mother.

"Thanks for reminding me, Paula!" Christy said, with enough sarcasm she hoped no one could tell how much it really bothered her.

"I'm only saying I learned from your experiences, Christy. So I wouldn't let my mom order me a new bathing suit from the Sears catalog before I came to California because I wanted to buy one here, like you did."

"Is that why Marti bought you all those clothes last summer?" Mom asked.

"Well," Christy hesitated. She had long struggled with the way her aunt so freely gave to her and yet also tried to control through the giving. "You know how Aunt Marti is, Mom. She likes things to be her way, and she's very generous."

I hope that came out okay. The last thing I want is for Paula to misquote me to my aunt!

"I can't wait to meet your sister, Mrs. Miller," Paula said, leaning forward in the seat to address Christy's mom. "I've heard so much about Aunt Marti I just know I'm going to like her. I can't wait to see their house. I've never known anyone who lived in a house right on the beach, and at Newport Beach too! Christy, you are so lucky! Is it very far from here? Where are we?"

"We're almost there," Christy's mom said and then asked Paula about how her mom and dad and all her family were. That filled the twenty minutes it took to arrive at Bob and

Marti's.

"There's never any parking here during the summer," Mom said with a sigh and then remembered, "Bob's in Maui, so I'll park in his usual spot in the driveway."

"Your uncle is in Maui? That's in Hawaii, isn't it? What am I saying? Of course it's in Hawaii . . . isn't it?"

"Yeah." David spoke up for the first time in an hour. "And Todd's there too! I wish I could've gone with them."

Mom pulled into the driveway and said to David with an unusually perky smile, "Watch what you wish for, son. You just might get it."

"Huh?" David said.

Mom turned off the ignition and was the first one out of the car, followed by Paula. Christy had to admit watching Paula experience the aura of the California beach life-style really was fun. Paula approached everything with a fresh excitement and delight.

"I'm so sure! Look at this house! Is this gorgeous or what? I can't believe this house! Is that your aunt there now?"

Aunt Marti, a slim, sophisticated woman who only slightly resembled Christy's mother, stepped out onto the front steps that were decorated with painted clay pots brimming with bright summer flowers. The blooms spilled over the sides and down the front walkway.

"So, this must be Paula!" Marti greeted them. "Welcome to California, darling. How was your flight?"

Marti gave each of them her usual feathery kiss on the cheek without smudging her lipstick or ruffling her short, dark hair.

"You always smell like flowers," David said when he got his kiss.

"Why, thank you, David," Marti said.

Before she could invite them inside, David turned to Mom and said, "Mom, you always smell like spaghetti sauce."

"Like spaghetti sauce!" A quick ocean breeze caught a curly bunch of Mom's short, dark hair and scattered it across her forehead. "What made you think of spaghetti sauce?"

Christy thought Mom looked a little hurt to be the "spaghetti sauce" next to her sister, who was the "flowers," even if Mom had grown used to such comparisons over the years.

"It's 'cuz Marti smells more like a garden, and you smell more like a kitchen."

"David, that is so rude!" Christy stopped his analogy, feeling bad for Mom. In a low voice between her teeth, she said, "I can't believe you'd say that!"

"Why?" David looked surprised. "I love spaghetti. It's just different from flowers, that's all."

Marti took the peculiar moment in her clever grasp and concluded, "I believe we have both been given a genuine compliment. They say the way to a man's heart is through his stomach! Now come in everyone, please."

They filed past Marti into the plush, modern-decor house. Paula took in everything as if this were a famous museum and responded with what Christy considered to be overly exaggerated ohhs and ahhs. Paula's exclamations continued into every room as Christy gave her the grand tour.

"Lunch is all ready and waiting in the kitchen," Marti

called up the stairs. Christy was showing Paula the guest room that had been her bedroom while she stayed with her aunt and uncle last summer. "I thought we'd be informal, so I picked up a few things at the deli."

Marti's "few things" turned out to be a full tray of various sliced meats, cheeses, relishes, four kinds of bread and a choice of three salads. David set to work immediately and built a sandwich so big Mom warned him he wouldn't be able to eat it all. And he couldn't.

"Can I go out on the beach?" David asked.

"Actually," Marti placed her diet soft drink down and looked at David with a serious expression, "I need to talk over something with you before you leave the table."

Christy thought something might be wrong, but when she looked at Mom, she had that perky little smile. As soon as she noticed Christy looking at her, Mom tried to put on a serious expression, but it didn't work.

"As you know," Marti began, "Bob is gone for several weeks and has left me all alone here."

Her dramatics reminded Christy of Paula's flair for animation. "It's really become more than I can bear, and so I've come to a decision."

David jumped up and spouted, "You want us to come stay here with you!"

Paula gasped and then entered in with the same enthusiasm. "Oh! Really? You'd let us all stay here with you? What a dream come true! I've always wanted to stay at a beach house!"

"No, no, no," Marti held up her hand and regained the

floor. "I am not inviting you to stay here."

"Oh," said Paula.

"Oh," said David, sitting back down.

Christy felt the same way inside, but she kept her reaction to herself.

"I'm not going to be here, so you can't stay with me here," Marti said. "But I would like you to stay with me on Maui!" This time she jumped up and opened her arms, waiting for the congratulatory hugs. Instead of trampling her, the three kids sat frozen in their seats, waiting for the punch line to what seemed like a joke.

"Didn't they hear me, Margaret?" Marti asked her sister.

Mom smiled and tried the direct approach. "Bob and Marti have invited us all to go to Maui. We leave in two days."

Paula screamed. She screamed so loud Christy put her fingers in her ears and let her mind replay Mom's words one more time. ". . . go to Maui. We leave in two days."

Marti received her awaited hugs from a screeching, jumping Paula and David. As soon as Christy let herself believe the announcement, she joined in the frolic.

When the noise died down, she heard Paula say, "You guys, I'm sure! This is just like winning on a TV game show or something! My mom is never going to believe this!"

"Your mom already knows," Christy's mom said. "I called and talked it over with her before you came out here."

"How long did you know, Mom?" Christy asked, feeling her heart steady itself from a wild sprint back to a jog.

"Oh, I don't know. A week or two. It was awfully hard keeping it a secret!"

"Does Dad know?" David asked.

"Yes, and that's something I haven't told you yet. Dad can't arrange to get off at the dairy, so he's not coming with us."

"He deserves a vacation more than any of us," Christy said.

"I know," Mom agreed.

Marti jumped in, "He said he'd come with us next time, and he even joked with Bob that the only reason we wanted him to go was to put him to work painting. Bob assured him that's why he was taking Todd along."

Todd! He must have known all along, because he kept saying we'd have a good time. No wonder he was laughing at me, that turkey!

This wasn't the first time Christy's aunt had arranged a special, extravagant surprise. It wasn't that Christy had grown accustomed to such treatment and no longer fully appreciated the special treats. She did. But the news of going to Maui didn't shock her the way it totally unnerved Paula.

"I'm so sure! I can't believe this! Can you believe this? I can't believe this!" Paula grabbed Christy and hugged her, squealing right in her ear. Then pulling herself out to arm's length, a horrified look came over Paula's face. "Oh, no! Oh, no!"

"What is it?" Marti asked, reaching over to pat Paula on the shoulder. "What's wrong?"

Paula turned around and moaned, "I won't have time to get a new bathing suit!"

Then Marti did something Christy had only seen a few times before. Marti laughed aloud. A real back-on-the-farm kind of laugh and said, "I should've known! You young girls are all alike! What do you think, Margaret? Why don't we take the rest of the afternoon and go shopping?"

"I guess we could do that."

"Aw, do we have to?" David griped. "Can't I just stay here on the beach?"

"In a few days you'll be on one of the most beautiful beaches in the world, David. Today, we shall go shopping!" Whenever Marti made declarations like that, David had learned better than to try to cross her. The girls were the first ones in the backseat of Marti's new silver car, which, Christy noticed, had more room than her old Mercedes and softer upholstery than she'd ever felt.

David wadded himself up by the left door, and when Marti started down the street, he played with the electric windows until Mom told him to stop. Paula began to talk the minute she slid into the backseat and didn't stop until they got to South Coast Plaza.

Marti took the car around to the valet parking, and Paula asked in amazement, "You mean you can hop out right here in front of the store, and somebody parks your car for you way down there, and you don't have to walk or anything? That's so cool. This is so unbelievable! Yesterday I was making frosty cones at the Dairy Queen, and today I'm shopping in California for my trip to Maui!"

She shrieked again and clutched Christy's arm. "When are you going to get excited about this trip and show some enthusiasm?"

"I *am* excited, Paula. It's just that you're expressing enough of it for both of us!"

"If the way you're acting now is your idea of enthusiasm, then it's no wonder you didn't make cheerleader!"

What a blow! Christy stopped walking, and Paula turned around and playfully said, "Aw, come on, Christy! Lighten up! I was just kidding!"

Why would Paula say such a thing? She knows I made the team but turned down the spot so another girl could take it. Why would Paula twist it like that and make me look bad?

Mom, Marti and David were walking ahead of them, but Christy felt sure they must have heard. It was hard not to hear Paula when she was cranked up.

Christy could feel a headache beginning to streak across the inside of her forehead. She wished she were taking a nap instead of participating in Marti's shopping parade.

Watching Paula's exuberance over the variety of bathing suits to choose from only made the situation worse. "Which one should I get, Christy?" Paula held up a neon green bikini on a hanger and modeled the same style in hot pink in the spacious dressing room.

"I don't care. Either one." Christy answered from her slouched position on the dressing room chair.

"Oh, well, you're a lot of help! Where's your aunt? I should ask her."

"She's still looking at stuff for my mom."

"I guess I'll get the green. I've never owned anything this bright in my life. I think I'll look more tan, don't you?"

"Yeah."

Paula took her eyes off her reflection and examined Christy. "Are you all right? You've been a total blob since we started shopping."

"I have a headache, and I feel kind of yucky."

"Why didn't you say so?" Paula said, springing into action and digging to the bottom of her huge purse. "Do you want real aspirin or Tylenol?" She pulled out a travel-size bottle of each.

"Look at you, Little Miss Organized!" Christy teased. "I'll take an aspirin. Just one. I need some water. I'll be right back."

Christy took the tablet and headed for where she'd seen a drinking fountain, glad for the excuse to get out of the dressing room. She knew it was a stupid little thing, and it shouldn't bother her, but the whole time she was helping Paula pick out a bathing suit, she felt waves of jealousy over Paula's figure.

To tall, lanky Christy, Paula seemed to have the perfect figure. She was just the right medium height and well proportioned, with a much larger bust than Christy's. Paula seemed proud of her figure, too, judging by the way she didn't hesitate to try on skimpy little bathing suits and model them without embarrassment.

I would never even try on that neon bathing suit! Christy thought as she sipped the cold water and swallowed the pill. *I'd never look as good as Paula does in a suit like that, but also, Mom would never let me out of the house with so little on.*

By the time Christy returned to the bathing suit department, Paula had paid for the swimsuit and stood waiting for her by the register with the bag in her hand.

"Did you get the green one?" Christy asked, trying to

hide her jealousy.

"Nope. Changed my mind. I got the pink one. Now I want to find some of those really cool sunglasses like I saw in a magazine that have the same color of hot pink on the sides. Do you think they have them here?"

"I think we better find my mom first," Christy suggested. "We can ask Marti about the sunglasses. She'd know where to find them."

"Aren't you going to get anything?" Paula asked.

"I don't know. Maybe. I can't really think of what I need."

"Forget what you need. Get what you want! I bet your aunt would buy anything you wanted if you just hinted you liked it."

"Yeah," Christy agreed, "she would."

What Christy didn't add was she'd tried that route with her aunt before, and it hadn't produced the kind of satisfaction she'd expected. Almost all of Aunt Marti's gifts came with a string attached, and Christy had concluded being content with what she had was more freeing than having lots of things and feeling like Marti's marionette.

"Girls!" Marti called. "Over here! Margie's getting a new bathing suit and cover-up. Did you two find anything?"

"Paula got a bathing suit too," Christy offered.

Marti looked at the bag in Paula's hand and with a slightly offended tone said, "You paid for it yourself?"

"Well, yeah," Paula answered, confused at Marti's reaction. "I planned on buying a suit once I got here, and I had the money all saved up and everything. It was even on sale!"

Marti handed her credit card to the clerk at the cash

register, and in a voice that sounded like a cooing dove, she said to Paula, "You tell me how much it was, and I'll give you the cash back. I wanted to get the swimsuit for you as my little welcome to California gift."

Paula's eyes stretched wide open, resembling two bright blue marbles. Christy thought she looked like a character in a storybook right after being sprinkled with fairy dust and told all her dreams were about to come true.

I didn't look that way last summer . . . did I?

They shopped another three hours, with David continually complaining until Marti bought him a frozen yogurt sundae in a waffle cone. Mom warned he wouldn't be able to finish it, and he didn't.

Paula spotted the sunglasses she wanted in a store window, and Marti swiftly bought them for her as well as a matching pair for Christy. Christy didn't even really like them. They were expensive, and she knew she should be appreciative to her aunt for the gift, so she said "thank you." But she refused to gush the way Paula did.

When the valet brought the car around, Marti suggested they go somewhere for dinner. Mom declined, saying she was anxious to get on the road since they still had another hour and a half drive back home to Escondido.

"Thank you soooooo much," Paula said, giving Marti a hug as they parted in Marti's driveway. "I love the sunglasses and the bathing suit and everything you got me. Thank you!"

"Thanks," Mom said, giving her sister a hug. "I guess we'll see you at six on Tuesday morning, when we pick you up."

"Right," Marti said efficiently. "Six at the latest because

the plane flies out at 8:30. Why don't you take the leftover lunch meat home for dinner? I won't eat it before we leave, and it's a waste to throw it out."

Mom followed Marti inside for the leftover deli tray, Christy and Paula transferred the shopping bags from Marti's car to Mom's car, and David claimed the front seat where he lined up his tiny cars on the dashboard.

"You sure didn't get much," Paula commented once the bags were all in the car. "How's your headache?"

"It's gone. Thanks for the aspirin."

"Can you believe we're going to Hawaii? I still can't believe it! And Todd is there! I can't wait to meet him! I noticed your bracelet while we were shopping. That must be the one he gave you on New Year's, right? And didn't he give it to you somewhere right around here, in the street? You'll have to show me the intersection on the way home. I thought that was so romantic when you wrote and told me all about him jumping out of the car and giving you the bracelet and kissing you and everything!"

"Ewwww!" David exclaimed. "You and Todd kissed? That's gross!"

Oh, good, Paula! Great! Thanks a lot. I'm so glad you feel free to make my private life public! Why did I ever tell you all those personal things?

Christy's expression mirrored her feelings, and Paula instantly got quiet while making a face that said "oops!" Then she giggled a tiny secret giggle like she and Christy had many times in the past. But this time the last thing Christy felt like doing was giggling.

All the way home Christy pretended to be asleep, with her head resting on the window. Paula didn't slow down a bit. She talked about the farm where Christy grew up and about the new owners while Mom kept her going with questions about a variety of people who lived in their small community.

Christy filtered it out and tried to figure out why she was feeling bothered by everything. This was Paula, her best friend ever since she could remember. They were going to Maui to spend a week with Todd.

She decided maybe she hadn't gotten enough sleep the night before. Whatever it was, she didn't like being so grumpy, and she decided to lighten up and try to act carefree like Paula.

I'm so sure, Christy! She tried out Paula's favorite phrase while mentally lecturing herself. *You're too uptight. Try to be perky like Paula. Paula's excited. You be excited too. Paula's cute. You try being cute too.*

With her eyes still closed and her head resting against the window, Christy pressed her lips together and forced them up into a puffy-cheeked, cutesy grin. She pictured herself opening her eyes, round and goggly like Paula's. Instead of seeing herself looking sweet and darling like Paula, the only image that came to her was Miss Piggy tilting her head and getting mushy over Kermit the Frog.

The picture struck Christy as so silly it actually chased away her foggy-headed feeling. The rest of the way home all she had to do was think, *Oh, Kermie, Kermie!* and a fresh little giggle bubbled up inside.

Chapter 3

If Only Katie Could Fit in My Suitcase

How odd it was, then, that when they got to Christy's house, Christy perked up and started being bubbly, while Paula took one look at their small, rented house and said, "This is where you live?" Then Paula became the moody one or tired one or whatever her problem was.

Dad suggested they order pizza since it was late. Then Mom wouldn't have to cook.

"Fine with me," Mom said. "Marti sent the rest of her deli tray home, so it looks like you can snack on leftovers for at least the first few days we're gone."

Dad didn't seem to mind they were all going without him. He listened to their exciting plans for Maui and said he'd go next time. He just had too much work at the Hollandale Dairy to take off right now.

In a way she couldn't explain, Christy admired her dad, watching him be happy for them without acting left out. She also knew Hawaii was not her dad's idea of the perfect vacation spot. He preferred a quiet lake and a fishing pole. They'd had many such camping vacations while she was growing up.

31

What she saw in her dad now was comforting. Something inside her said, "Even though my dad isn't a Hawaiian-vacation kind of person, he doesn't try to stop us from going."

David ate three pieces of pizza, leaving all the bell peppers on his plate. Paula barely nibbled on one piece before saying she felt tired.

"I'll bet you are," Dad said. "It's half past midnight where you come from. I put the roll-away in Christy's room for you. It's a tight squeeze, so don't try to open the door all the way."

Christy showed Paula where the towels were in the bathroom. At her friend's request, she came up with an extra pillow for her and then got ready for bed while Paula occupied the bathroom.

When Paula returned to Christy's room, she found Christy lying on her bed reading her Bible.

"What are you reading?" Paula asked.

"My Bible."

"You're kidding. Do you do that all the time now?" Paula tossed her dirty clothes in the corner of the bedroom.

"Well, I try to everyday. Even if it's only a little bit."

Paula responded with an "oh." Then she slipped into her roll-away bed, fluffed up the pillows and turned her back to Christy.

A few minutes later, Christy heard a huge yawn followed by, "Are you going to turn out the light pretty soon? Not to be rude or anything, but I'm really, really tired."

"Oh, sure." Christy obliged, closing her Bible and

snapping off the light. "Sweet dreams, Paula! Dream about Maui—the golden beaches, the summer sun, the clear blue water . . . Paula?"

The only sound coming from Paula was the deep breathing of a sound sleep.

Christy stretched out under the covers, folding her hands behind her head and facing the dark bedroom ceiling. Then in a whisper, with her lips moving but no sound emerging, Christy prayed.

"Lord, I have to tell her about You, but I don't know how. I've told her in letters, and last summer I told her how I gave my life to You and promised You my whole heart.

"But she doesn't understand. I feel as though we're so different now, Paula and me. There's so little between us that's the same, and before we were like twin sisters.

"I think that's why I was so bummed out today. I wanted to be close to her like I used to be, but we've both changed too much.

"She needs to become a Christian, like me, and then we can be close again. I'm going to try everything I can to show her she needs to give her life to You.

"Oh, and Lord, thanks for working out everything so that we could go to Maui. Please be with Todd right now and keep him safe. Good night, Lord."

Before she could add "amen," Christy drifted off into a beach-and-surf island dream.

The July morning sun hit Christy's window at 6:20 and flooded the room with light through her thin, lacy, white curtains. Christy had adapted all summer by pulling the

covers over her head and hovering between the real world
and dreamland for at least another hour.

Paula, however, wasn't the hovering type. She greeted
the early morning sun by opening the bedroom window and
unpacking her suitcase, singing softly to herself.

"What are you doing?" Christy asked the early bird.

"You're awake! Good! Why don't you get up and give
me your opinion on which clothes I should take to Hawaii
and which ones I should leave here. Remember, your aunt
said we should try to take only one suitcase each. I have too
much stuff, so I have to decide what I really need and what I
don't. Is it always hot in Hawaii? Or should I take jeans
and sweatshirts?"

Christy pulled the covers over her head and mumbled, "I
can't believe you're up! Do you know what time it is?"

Paula pulled a watch out of her large purse. "In
Wisconsin it's almost ten. I'd be getting ready for work
right now if I was home, but I'm not! I'm in California, and
tomorrow we're going to Maui."

Christy rolled over and pulled back the covers from her
eyes. "You mean that wasn't just an exotic dream I had last
night? We really are going to Hawaii?"

Paula laughed and tossed a pillow at her. "I know! I still
can't believe it either. This is going to be the absolute best
summer of my whole life! But wait a minute."

Paula plopped herself down next to Christy's legs at the
end of her bed and said, "You haven't told me anything at all
about Todd since I've been here. I thought you'd be going
on about him nonstop like you do in your letters."

Christy propped herself up on her elbow and said, "I haven't exactly had a chance to tell you much. I mean, I'm not exactly into telling my whole life story in front of my little brother, like some people I know!"

She flung back the pillow at Paula. Paula caught it, hugged it to her middle and giggled. "Sorry about that! It's probably good for David to realize that people, you know, kiss and stuff. He's old enough to figure all that out, isn't he?"

"I don't think so. Besides, Todd is like a big brother or a cousin to David. Sometimes I think he spends more time with Todd than I do!"

"So, tell me everything. I've been dying to hear. Are you in love?"

Christy laughed.

"Come on!" Paula urged. "This is pillow-talk time. How far have you guys gone?"

"What do you mean?" Christy asked, scooting up and leaning against her pillow.

"You know. How far have you gone? Like kissing and everything."

"Well, he's kissed me about five times."

"And?"

"And what?"

"What else?" Paula nudged Christy's feet with her elbow.

"That's all. There is nothing else."

Paula stared at Christy a second, and then, as if convinced she was telling the truth, pulled back and said, "Then something's wrong."

"What do you mean?"

"Think about it, Christy! You guys have known each other for more than a year, and you've pretty much been going together the whole time, right?"

"We're not exactly going together."

"You're not going out with anyone else, are you?"

"Of course not! Paula, you know I'm not really allowed to date until I'm sixteen."

"I'll bet you anything Todd is going out with someone else."

Christy gave Paula a slightly disgusted look and tried to figure out what Paula could be getting at.

"You don't see it, do you? Christy! How could you be so blind? When a guy likes you, he does more than just kiss you, and more than five times in a year! If Todd really, truly loved you, he'd be much more, you know, aggressive. That's how you can tell if a guy really likes you—by how hard he comes after you. He's probably got another girlfriend in Newport Beach, and you're just like the back-up, girl-next-door, good friend kind of girlfriend."

Christy knew Paula was wrong, but she didn't feel quite awake enough to try to prove it. She'd heard these kinds of accusations from another friend months ago. The other girl's words had awakened a fear and anxiety in Christy over Todd. She'd since become more secure in her relationship with him, even if their relationship didn't fit anyone else's idea of "normal."

"You know," Paula concluded, adjusting her position at the end of the bed. "I'm pretty surprised. All along I thought you guys were a whole lot more serious, and you just weren't writing it in your letters in case your mom or my mom read them."

"Paula, wait until you meet Todd. He's not like any other guy. He would never try to push our relationship into anything more than what it is. Physically, or otherwise. That's just the kind of guy he is."

"There is no such guy!" Paula declared. "No eighteen-year-old guy, who is as good looking and wonderful as you say he is, is going to limit himself to only one girl. I still say he has another girlfriend he hasn't told you about."

Christy shook her head. "Wait until you meet him, Paula. You'll see. He's a Christian. He really loves the Lord."

As soon as Christy mentioned "the Lord," Paula ended the conversation by heading for the bathroom to get ready for the day. Christy tried to snuggle back down and get some more sleep.

Too late. Her brain functioned at full speed, sorting through everything Paula said and throwing out most of it.

It did occur to Christy, though, that Paula had drilled her for details about her boyfriend, yet Paula hadn't volunteered one word about any of the guys she'd mentioned in her letters over the past year.

When Paula returned to the bedroom, Christy asked, "You didn't tell me if you have a boyfriend or not. What happened to that one guy? I forgot his name. Wasn't he Melissa's brother?"

"Him?" Paula looked surprised Christy would ask. "No, he's long gone. I don't have a boyfriend. I wanted to come to California available for all the surfers I thought you were going to introduce me to!"

She looked cute and playful when she said, "Now I guess I'll have to settle for a Hawaiian surfer."

Christy's mom appeared in the hallway and stuck her head into the girls' room, saying, "I thought I heard you girls up. Ready for some breakfast?"

That stopped the talk about guys until that afternoon when Christy's redheaded friend, Katie, came over. Paula and Christy were in Christy's room packing when they suddenly heard a cheery voice say, "Okay, tell me David is great at making up fairy tales, and I'll save myself a couple of bucks."

"Katie! Hi!" Christy said. "This is Paula. Paula, this is Katie."

"Hi."

"Hi."

"So, what did my brother do this time?"

Katie leaned against the door, her green eyes flashing from Paula back to Christy. "Dear David gave me some fairy tale about you guys going to Maui tomorrow. When I told him I didn't believe him, he made me agree if he was telling the truth, I'd have to buy him an ice cream cone. So tell me he's a confused little kid, living in a fantasy world."

"He is," Christy said quickly. "But he's also telling the truth. It's one of my aunt's little surprises. We leave tomorrow morning."

From the hallway they could hear David chanting, "I told you so, I told you so!"

"I can't believe it! Do you guys realize how lucky you

are?"

"I know!" Paula jumped in and rattled off all the details to a straight-faced Katie, who had lowered herself onto a corner of the roll-away bed and sat still, taking in the whole story.

Christy felt awkward. She thought how much it must hurt Katie that Paula had suddenly showed up and taken her place as Christy's closest friend. And now they were preparing to whisk away to paradise and leave Katie behind.

Christy felt especially uncomfortable because last fall Marti had taken her and two other girls to Palm Springs, and Katie couldn't go along because of her obligations as school mascot. The trip had turned into a disaster, and Christy now rarely even saw the girls she'd invited along on that adventure. But she'd promised Katie after the Palm Springs trip she'd invite her along on the next trip Marti set up, no matter where they were going.

And now here the whole Hawaii trip had been planned to include Paula, and Katie hadn't even been told they were going. Christy knew Katie would understand later when she got a chance to explain everything in private. She couldn't attempt to explain things now without offending Paula, especially if it came out sounding like Christy would rather have taken Katie than her.

"That's pretty incredible," Katie exclaimed when Paula finished the exciting account. "I hope you guys have a good time. I sure wish I were going with you!"

Now Christy felt even worse. Those were the same things she'd said to Todd the morning he'd left. But she didn't have any secrets up her sleeve like Todd had.

For one instant, Christy considered asking her mom if she could call Aunt Marti and see if Katie could somehow come too. She threw the idea out when a mental picture of Mom's face appeared. Christy knew Mom would never let her ask such an expensive favor, and besides, she'd vowed long ago to never again beg her aunt for anything.

"I came over to see if you both wanted to come spend the night while Paula was here, but it looks like your social calendar is filling up too fast for me." Katie said it good-naturedly, and Christy admired her for it.

"We're only going to be gone a week," Christy suggested. "Maybe we could get together when we get back before Paula goes home."

"Sure," Katie agreed. "Bring back some grass skirts, and we'll have an all-night hula contest."

They all laughed, and then Katie graciously offered to help them pack. She pitched in with a sweet attitude.

Katie, you amaze me. If I were you, I'd be on my way home, crying by now. You are the kind of friend I want to be.

"What do you think?" Paula asked Katie. "Is it always hot there, or should I take some sweatshirts?"

"I guess take one sweatshirt, just in case."

"Then which one? I brought three. They're all university ones. Whenever I wear them people come up and ask if I go there, like to Michigan State or whatever. So what do you think is the coolest university to be identified with in Hawaii?" Paula laid out her three sweatshirts.

"Whichever one is the farthest away," Katie suggested.

"You know, it makes you look like you came a long way to see the islands."

"I did come a long way," Paula returned.

"Then wear the Wisconsin one and be true to your home state."

"But the colors in the Pennsylvania one match more of my clothes," Paula said, eyeing the three displayed sweatshirts.

"All I know," Christy said, folding a pair of shorts, "is you'd better decide, Paula. We are leaving in the morning, you know!"

"Taking your tennis shoes, Christy?" Katie asked, bringing over a pair from the closet.

"I guess so. Are you Paula?"

"We'd better; in case we go jogging. Jogging is a great way to meet guys, you know."

"I'll remember that," Katie said, laughing at Paula's serious advice. She placed Christy's tennis shoes in the bottom of her suitcase and offered her own advice. "I always put my shoes and Bible in the bottom since they're the heaviest things."

"Good idea," Christy said, fitting her cloth-covered Bible in next to her shoes like she was putting together a puzzle.

"You know," Katie said, her fair-skinned face becoming sober, "I think it's really a God-thing that you get to go to Maui."

"A 'God-thing'?" Paula asked with a laugh. "What's that?"

Katie remained serious, which didn't happen too often.

"It's when something happens in your life, and you look at it and can't explain how or why it happened, but you know there's a reason for it. You know that God is doing something in your life, and it changes you. There's no other way to explain it except to see it as a God-thing."

"We know why this happened, though," Paula quickly responded. "It's because Christy's aunt invited us to go with her."

"Yeah, but think about it. How many people do you know who get invited to Hawaii, all expenses paid?" Katie asked. "Don't you think it's a God-thing, Christy? I think God's going to do something in both of your lives while you're over there."

Christy wasn't sure what a God-thing was supposed to be, but she appreciated Katie's encouraging words. They were like a blessing from someone who could have felt hurt or left out.

A little bit later, when Paula went to the kitchen for something to drink, Katie continued her thought. "Don't you think it's a God-thing, Christy? I mean, I know how long you've been waiting for Paula to come visit, and I know how you've been praying that she'd become a Christian. If you ask me, this whole trip is set up so that you and Todd can witness to Paula. Isn't that kind of how you became a Christian last summer? From hearing about the Lord from Todd and another girl?"

"Sort of. Her name was Tracy. But it wasn't so much what they said; it was more what they were. Todd and Tracy both had something I didn't and that's what got me the most."

"But didn't they both witness to you, together? I thought that's what you told me one time when you showed me your Bible. Didn't they both give you your Bible?"

"Yeah, but, I don't know. It wasn't like they told me about the Lord, and I said, 'Okay, sure I'd like to give my life to Christ.' It was more like they kept telling me in different ways I needed the Lord. I kind of ignored them. At first. Then later everything they'd been saying, along with some other stuff that had happened, hit me really hard. I knew I had to make a decision."

Katie's green eyes were serious as she said, "You know what I think? I think you shouldn't get discouraged if Paula doesn't hear you and Todd or understand right away when you talk about Jesus. You've got to give it time."

"I know, I know." Christy couldn't explain it, but she felt irritated by Katie's advice. Realizing she must sound rude, she added, "Just pray for us, okay?"

"I will," Katie said. "I promise. And I still think this trip is a God-thing."

After Katie left, Paula made fun of the way she had called their trip a God-thing. "Don't you get freaked out around people who talk about God like He was, you know, a Spirit watching over you or something?"

"Well, He kind of is, Paula," Christy began, hoping for a chance to explain. "I think what Katie meant—"

Paula cut her off. "Oh, you don't have to defend her, Christy. I like Katie. I think she's really nice. I'm just saying she seemed great until she got all mystical on us."

Just then Mom poked her head in the room. "You girls all

packed? I hope you managed to get it all into one suitcase each."

"Just about," Christy said, surveying her neatly packed suitcase. "All I need to do is put in my cosmetic bag in the morning."

Mom stepped closer to examine their packing job. A hot pink string hung out of the side of Paula's packed but not yet closed suitcase. Mom tugged on the string until the rest of the bikini top popped out.

"Oh my!" was all Mom said. She kept holding it up as if she were trying to figure out what to do with it. "Is this yours, Paula?"

"Yes," Paula answered politely and without expressing any of the embarrassment Christy felt.

"Is this the swimsuit you bought yesterday?"

"Yeah." Paula plucked the small top from Mrs. Miller's hand and crammed it back into her suitcase, making sure all the strings were tucked in this time.

"Paula," Mom began diplomatically, "I'm not sure your mother would approve of that suit."

Look out, Paula! Here it comes!

Christy struggled with her feelings for both sides. If she could get up the nerve or had the right kind of figure, she'd probably want to wear a hot pink bikini too. Still, she knew her mom was about to appeal for the side of modesty, and she agreed with that side too.

"Oh, don't worry, Mrs. Miller. I only bought this one to sunbathe in. I have my old one-piece for swimming. I bought this one because, I mean, what's the point of going to

Hawaii if you can't come home really tan?"

Mom seemed satisfied with Paula's reasoning and only gave her a warning. "I'd like you to make sure you have a T-shirt or cover-up along so you can slip it on in case you're sunbathing and the guys show up."

Paula smiled her agreement, and Mom let it go at that. She urged the girls to get to bed early since they'd be leaving at four in the morning for the airport. Christy couldn't help but think if she ever tried to bring home a bikini, her mom and dad would forbid her to ever wear it—for sunbathing or anything. Paula had gotten off easy.

Paula fell asleep quickly again that night, while Christy kept finding little things to finish up or stick into her suitcase, which she did in the dim light from the hallway so as not to disturb Paula. One of the things Christy came across as she cleaned off her desk was the mysterious letter she'd received a few days ago. She stuck it in her purse, intending to ask Paula the next morning if she'd written it. And what did the part, "I thought about what you said," mean?

Christy glanced around her room in the faint light and felt pleased she was leaving everything basically neat. She liked having things where she could find them.

The only thing left to clear away was the mound of dirty clothes the two girls had been tossing into the corner for the last two days. Christy scooped it up and carried it down to the washing machine in the garage.

As she dumped it on top of the washing machine, she saw Paula's one-piece bathing suit wadded up and tucked in with the other dirty clothes. Christy tried to figure out why Paula would put her bathing suit in the wash, especially after telling Mom she planned to wear it while swimming instead of her new bikini.

She must have accidently tossed it in the corner when she was sorting out her clothes. Or, could it be that Paula was trying to hide the suit and leave it at Christy's so when she got to Maui she'd have no choice but to wear the bikini the whole time?

Christy leaned against the cold washing machine and thought how the Paula she grew up with would never do something deceptive like that. Trouble was, Paula had changed. Christy wasn't sure who this new Paula was or what she might be capable of.

Chapter 4

Flight 272 Is Now Boarding

Here today, gone to Maui!" David said for about the fifteenth time as Mom drove the car along the freeway. It was almost six o'clock, and Christy knew they'd be late picking up Marti. That would make Marti mad, and if they missed their flight, that would make everyone mad.

"All right, David," Mom snapped. "That's the last time I want to hear you say that, understand?"

He nodded and wisely kept quiet. Mom didn't get ruffled often, but when she did, look out.

Christy exercised the same prudence and kept her mouth shut, feeling the tension Mom displayed by clutching the steering wheel tightly and driving close to the car in front of them. They'd left home when it was still dark, but now the day was wide awake, and the freeway crowded with vacationers and commuters.

"Come on, come on," Mom muttered to the motor home in front of them. "Either speed up or move it over, buddy."

Christy had rarely heard her mom talk to other motorists, and she thought it was kind of funny.

"My mom does that all the time too. Talks to cars, I

mean," Paula told Christy in the backseat, where they sat with a big duffle bag between them. "It cracks me up. She really gets upset at tractors on the road. I just pass them, but my mom follows them for miles. It's so funny."

"You have your license already?" Christy asked.

"No, just my permit. But I drive all the time anyway. Everyone does."

"What about the insurance? What if you got in an accident?"

"I don't know."

"You're kidding!" Christy looked at bright-eyed Paula. "Insurance is a big deal here. Nobody can drive without insurance, and it's super expensive. My Uncle Bob said he'd pay my insurance for the first year if I passed my driver's test the first time I tried."

David turned around and announced, "And she needs insurance! She already had an accident!"

"You did? What happened?" Paula quizzed her.

Christy gave her brother a dirty look before explaining the parking lot incident in a matter-of-fact way, hoping it would come across as no big deal.

Paula giggled. "That must've been embarrassing! Did anyone see you do it?"

"No, just my dad."

"So, did you get your license yet?"

"I haven't taken the test yet. My birthday's not until . . ." Christy's eyes grew big and bright. "I can't believe it! I almost forgot all about my birthday!"

"Hey," Paula added, "it's tomorrow, isn't it? With all the

Hawaii stuff, I almost forgot too. I'm so sure! You're going to spend your sixteenth birthday in Hawaii. Is that like a dream, or what?"

"You may end up spending your sixteenth birthday in this car, if that motor home doesn't move it!" Mom sputtered.

Christy and Paula turned and made giggly faces at each other, laughing at Mom's anxiety attack. A few minutes later they spotted the reason for the clogged freeway—a stalled truck had closed off the center lane, and traffic had been routed around on both sides.

Once they made it past the holdup, the freeway cleared, but the tension kept building until they reached Marti's. Then the fireworks really began. Christy and Paula watched as the two women acted like teenage sisters, squabbling over why Mom was fifteen minutes late, which car they should take, and why they couldn't have been more organized.

The group ended up in Mom's car, with David in the backseat, his seatbelt tightly holding both him and the duffle bag, and Marti in the front seat with a suitcase under her feet.

"This is precisely why I requested you each fit your things into one suitcase apiece," Marti scolded. "This day is certainly starting out wrong; I've never left so late for a flight in my life!"

"We hit a lot of traffic, and there was a stalled truck," Mom explained, still gripping the steering wheel tightly as she maneuvered back onto the freeway.

"We might be able to bypass some of the traffic," Marti suggested, "if we get on the 405. See the sign there? Stay in this lane."

Mom followed the directions while Marti continued to make plans. "Okay, now, if we do miss our flight, which I certainly hope we don't, then we'll find out when the next flight leaves and switch to that."

As it turned out, they didn't need Marti's alternative. They made it to the airport, checked their luggage, received their seat assignments and ended up with half an hour before they could even board the plane. Mom gave in to David's pleas for a pack of gum, and the two of them scurried off to the nearest shop, leaving a somewhat subdued Marti sitting in the waiting area with the girls.

"We should've gone with them," Paula suggested after Mom and David were out of view. "I don't have any gum, and my ears always bother me on airplanes."

"Paula," Christy pointed out, "you've only been on one airplane in your whole life and that was a few days ago coming out here."

"I know. And I chewed gum the whole time. Marti, would it be okay if we went to get some gum?"

"I suppose. If you hurry. I'll stay here with the carryons. Don't forget, we board in less than half an hour."

"Would you like us to bring you anything?" Paula asked sweetly.

"No thanks, dear. Just hurry!"

Paula and Christy briskly nudged their way through a throng of people lined up at the check-in desk. Christy suggested they make a quick stop at the bathroom too, since Marti had said the flight would take five hours.

"First some gum," Paula directed. "And I saw a

magazine I wanted to get while we were running past all those shops on the way in."

Suddenly Paula stopped. "I don't believe it!" she squealed under her breath, or as under her breath as Paula was capable of squealing. Then plunging her hand deep into her huge shoulder bag, she rummaged around until she pulled out a pair of glasses, which she quickly slipped on.

"When did you start to wear glasses?" Christy asked.

"That's him! Over there; see him? That's the guy from that TV show—what's that show? You know, there's these two guys and—"

Grabbing Christy by the arm Paula yanked her around the bathroom area and into another section of the terminal. "Come on! He's going this way! Did you see him? What's his name, Christy? I can't remember his name!"

"Paula!" Christy yanked her arm back and yelled at her friend, "Paula!"

Paula turned, looking dazed but still heading toward the movie star. "What? What! Come on!"

Christy hustled to keep up with her. "I don't see who you're even talking about! Come on, Paula! What are you doing?"

"I'm going to get my first movie star's autograph! Come on!"

They blitzed past a large tour group and ended up in a section of the airport that had two wings to choose from.

"This one." Paula grabbed Christy by the arm again. "I saw him go this way."

"Paula! Do you even know who we're chasing?"

"I can't think of his name. He's on that show, you know . . ."

Paula stopped short. "Where did he go? I don't see him!"

"Paula, I mean it! We have to go back right now! I didn't see anybody who looked famous. This is stupid!" Christy brimmed with anger and exasperation but kept her words brief. "We have to go back right now!"

She abruptly turned and marched away from Paula.

"Okay, okay, I'm coming." Paula caught up. "I know I saw him, though. What's his name? This is going to drive me crazy! He's really cute and popular and he's on that show . . ."

"Most movie stars are cute and popular and on shows!" Christy picked up her pace, scolding Paula over her shoulder. "I can't believe you! We could've gotten lost or missed our plane over this phantom movie star!"

"Wait, Christy," Paula urged, slipping her glasses back into the bag and grabbing Christy's arm again, which Christy jerked away. "I want to go in here and get some gum."

"We don't have time!"

"Yes, we do. Your aunt was just pressuring everybody. We have like an hour until the plane takes off."

"Half an hour," Christy corrected.

"Half an hour till we board; then it takes another half hour until the plane even takes off. We have plenty of time."

Paula entered the small souvenir shop and took her time browsing through the magazines before selecting one. She picked up a pack of gum and held it up for Christy to see. "You like this kind?"

"I don't care. Anything. Let's go!"

Paula slipped her purchases into her bag, and the two girls stepped back into the main terminal area and looked around. Neither of them moved. Nothing looked familiar.

"We go this way," Paula said, regaining her self-assurance.

"Are you sure? I thought our gate was over there."

A cloud of uncertainty came over Paula, casting a puzzled shadow on her expression and giving away her feelings of terror.

The noise and constant hubbub from the throngs of people rushing past them made Christy feel dizzy.

"Let's ask somebody," Paula said breathlessly, scanning the bustling crowd, apparently looking for a stranger who appeared approachable and trustworthy.

"We can't just start talking to some stranger!"

"Then what are we going to do?" Paula dug her fingernails into Christy's arm, sounding as panicked as she looked. "What are we going to do? We're lost!"

"Let go!" Christy said. "Where's one of those TV monitors that shows all the flights and their times?"

"Over there!" Paula spotted one on the wall behind them. "What flight are we on? What airline? Do you know? I don't even know what airline we're on!"

"It was United, wasn't it?" Christy asked, as they scrambled closer to the monitor for a better view.

"There!" Paula said pointing. "Honolulu! There's a flight in half an hour to Honolulu. That's us, isn't it? Honolulu is in Hawaii, isn't it? Of course it is. Isn't it?" Her voice rose and became squeakier.

"Yes! Yes! Yes!" Christy's irritation overtook her fear. "But what's the one listed above it? How do you say that—

Ka-hu-lu-i?" Christy asked. "I think that's the airport we're going to because that one leaves at the time we were supposed to, and it has a Hawaiian name."

"How do you know it's a Hawaiian name? Honolulu—now that's a Hawaiian name. Kahului could be some place in Bora Bora, or worse, it could be a flight to the Antarctic! We can't go jumping on the first flight we find that has a Hawaiian-sounding name! I think we should go to Gate 87 where the flight to Honolulu is. Everyone knows Honolulu is in Hawaii."

Just then the Kahului line began to blink, and instead of a time being listed, the words "now boarding" flashed across the screen.

"Now boarding, Paula! I know that's our flight! I know it! And they're leaving right now. Come on! Gate 57. Where's Gate 57?"

The girls took off sprinting down the nearest wing of the terminal, then realized it was the wrong one and ran the other way, following signs and bumping into people. Both of them were crying. Panting and blinking wildly, they suddenly recognized the wing they'd started from.

"This is it! I'm sure of it," Christy said, and the girls dashed to the waiting area which previously had been crowded with people. It was empty now, except for Christy's mother, who had her back to them. She stood next to the ticket counter, talking to the flight attendant and using sharp hand motions.

"Mom!" Christy yelled from twenty yards back, not caring who heard her. "Mom!"

"Mrs. Miller!" Paula screeched.

Mom spun around, and instead of welcoming them with a relieved embrace, she planted both fists on her hips. Her face, stern as stone, told Christy everything she didn't want to know.

"We missed the plane, girls," Mom stated. "We missed the plane! Where have you been?"

Christy scrambled to gain her composure and respond as maturely as possible. Before she could say a word, Paula let her emotions rip. With wild sobs, she clung to Mom's arm and went on hysterically about trying to get away from some strange man and getting lost and being afraid the man was going to kidnap them and a whole bunch of other unintelligible garble.

Mom instantly changed her approach and tried to calm Paula down before she drew a crowd. Christy kept all her terrified feelings from being lost to herself and wiped away her tears.

"Excuse me," the flight attendant interjected, leaning over the counter and looking much sweeter and more concerned than she had when Mom had been talking with her a few minutes ago. "Are you girls okay?"

Christy nodded.

Paula could have landed a role in a melodrama with her reaction. She curled in her lower lip, opened her eyes wide and let more inky, mascara-stained tears zigzag down her baby face.

Then softly, to Christy's mom, the uniformed woman said, "We did experience an abduction of an eight-year-old girl at the airport last Thursday. Perhaps I should call security."

"No!" Paula said quickly. "I mean, it would take too

long. We already missed our flight, and it would take too long to answer all the questions and everything."

"We're okay," Christy added. "Nothing really happened. We got lost. That's all." No one seemed to believe Christy's mild account.

"Let me check on something," the woman said, lifting the phone and holding it in place with her shoulder while typing something on her computer keyboard.

"Mrs. Miller," she said in a professional tone, "why don't you and your daughters have a seat. I'll let you know what I can find out here."

The three of them moved over to the waiting-area seats, and Mom pulled out some tissue from her purse for the girls. "You sure you're all right?"

They both nodded and blew their noses. Christy said, "Mom, I'm really sorry. We got lost, and—"

"It's okay, honey. Marti and David boarded the flight, and I had you paged. I also tried to get us on another flight, but they're all booked. Right before you came up, the gal was telling me the best we could get would be three seats on a flight leaving tomorrow night."

"Tomorrow night!" Paula wailed and began to cry all over again.

"That's my birthday!" Christy bleated, joining Paula in another round of tears.

Just then a security guard drove up in a tan, motorized cart and said, "Mrs. Miller? Would you like to get in? I'll drive you to the gate."

Mom looked questioningly at him. The woman at the

desk then slipped out from her spot behind the computer and placed a tender hand on Paula's shoulder.

She explained, "I've cleared three seats for you on another carrier. You'll have to change planes in Honolulu and take Aloha Airlines' Flight 210 into Kahului."

She handed Mom some tickets and pointed to the handwritten information at the top of the packet. "Make sure you give them this code number when you check in on both flights. It's very important you show them this number."

She turned and smiled sympathetically at the girls. "You two look out for each other on your vacation now, okay?"

Before any of them fully realized what had happened, they were seated on the cart and whisked away through the crowds to the other side of the terminal. Mom showed the tickets and the special code number, and they were immediately ushered onto a waiting plane and given three seats in first class.

People looked at them, and the flight attendants treated them like royalty. In a few minutes, they had their seat belts on, and the plane was taxiing down the runway. The roar of the engines matched the roar of emotions revving up inside Christy.

She leaned over and whispered to Paula, who was watching the smoggy world miniaturize below them, "Why do you think they treated us like that?"

"It must've been because of the abduction thing. They thought we had been chased by a kidnapper."

"But, Paula, that's not what happened at all! They thought that because you made it sound that way."

"Well, I was scared!"

"I was too!" Christy countered. "You shouldn't have lied, though."

"I didn't really lie, Christy." Paula looked offended.

Christy clenched her teeth and gave Paula a serious look.

Paula broke into a big smile and breathed a lighthearted laugh. "Relax, Christy, will you? I'm so sure! You should see yourself right now! You look like that old prune-faced lady who used to work at the post office. What was her name?"

Christy was not pleased with the analogy. The prune-faced lady at the post office, a lady whose glares had frightened her as a child, was not a person she wanted to remember and definitely not a person she ever wanted to resemble.

"Besides, I don't much remember what I said." Paula reached for her headphones and began to untangle the cord. "Everything turned out fine, so I think it's best if we just don't say any more about it, okay?"

"It isn't right, Paula. It's deceitful."

"Why? Nobody was hurt, and we didn't get in trouble. Actually, it turned out great. If we hadn't been crying and frightened and everything, they certainly wouldn't have given us all the special treatment. They never would have put us on this flight, and we wouldn't have left until tomorrow night. Think about it, Christy. Would you like to spend your birthday at an airport or on the beach?"

"On the beach, of course, but—"

"Then give it a rest!" Paula interrupted, confidently reclining the plush, first-class seat and popping her headphones into place. "Face it, Christy. This is what your friend Katie would call a God-thing."

Chapter 5

Aloha!

Five hours in an airplane is long enough for anyone to "give it a rest." Christy pretty much decided to put the whole morning ordeal behind her. She couldn't convince herself, like Paula had, that the "happy" ending to their run through the airport was a God-thing. But she certainly didn't want the rest of the trip to turn into one, big, ongoing emotional battle with Paula.

So Christy decided, right before they landed in Honolulu, she'd have to do everything she could to show Paula the difference between right and wrong, truth and lies. After all, she was a Christian, and Paula wasn't.

The first thing Christy noticed when they deplaned was how sweet the air smelled. It was midday when they arrived, and the air felt warm and balmy. She'd expected that from the movies she'd seen and from her idea of what tropical weather felt like.

But the flower-scent dancing in the air was unexpected. The wonderful fragrance came from young, Polynesian women dressed in tropical attire, their arms looped with fragrant leis, who greeted certain travelers as they exited.

Following the many signs, the girls trotted after Mom, who led them directly to the Aloha Airlines booth and presented the flight transfer papers she'd been issued in Los Angeles. They were ushered within minutes onto a nearly full plane and were barely in their seats before the plane took off.

"That was a tight connection!" Mom said, twisting around in her seat to talk to Christy. "Marti and David flew directly to Maui. We're only about a hour behind them. Maybe a little less."

"Look how clear the water is," Paula remarked, as they soared over the Pacific Ocean. "You can almost see to the bottom."

"Alissa used to live here," Christy said, "and she told me the water is really warm."

"Who's Alissa?"

During their quick island-hop to Maui, Christy told Paula about Alissa, the gorgeous girl Christy met on Newport Beach last summer. Christy had thought Alissa had a lot going for her, but she had gotten involved with a bunch of guys, one of whom was Todd's best friend, Shawn.

"You mean Shawn, the one who died last summer in that surfing accident?" Paula asked.

"Yeah."

"Wasn't he on drugs or something?"

"It's a long story, but, yeah, he'd been smoking dope."

"And this guy was Todd's best friend?"

Christy nodded and continued. "Anyway, Shawn and Alissa were together for a while during the summer, if you know what I mean."

Christy spoke softly, not sure how much of this her mom might overhear. Paula leaned closer, waiting for Christy to finish the story.

"Well, Alissa got pregnant, and she had a baby girl last spring. She named it Shawna Christy because of, well, you know, because Shawn was the father, and Christy because we were kind of friends."

"And she kept the baby?"

"Last I heard she was going to try to raise it on her own."

"If that ever happened to me, I'd give up the baby for adoption," Paula said matter-of-factly. "Wouldn't you?"

"I don't plan to ever be in that situation!"

"Nobody ever plans to be in that situation, Christy. It just happens."

Christy lowered her voice even more, though inside she felt like raising her voice. "It's not going to 'just happen' to me. I'm not going to bed with a guy until our wedding night. I won't have to worry about it 'just happening.' "

"I used to think that too," Paula said wistfully, looking out the window. Then she turned to face Christy, and with a mist rolling over her ocean-blue eyes, she spoke softly, "I'm the only virgin I know, Christy. Except for you."

"Oh, come on."

"I'm serious. Of all the girls I hang around with, I'm the only one. Do you know what a freak they think I am? If I don't get a boyfriend during this trip . . ." Her voice trailed off, and she turned her gaze back out the plane window, ending the discussion.

Christy pressed her back into the seat and let Paula's

words sink in. She couldn't believe Paula had changed so much that she now couldn't wait to give away her virginity so she'd fit in with her friends. Christy had become close to a group of Christian girls during the past school year, and all of them seemed to be trying as hard to keep their virginity as Paula and her friends were trying to give theirs away.

More than anything else that had happened on this trip, the last few sentences from Paula hit Christy like a gust of wind, strong enough to bend her opinion of her lifelong friend. She didn't want to see Paula turn out like Alissa.

The pilot's calm voice came over the sound system, announcing their arrival. "We are now beginning our descent into Kahului, Maui, International Airport. The time is 1:20, and the temperature is a balmy eighty-six degrees. We hope you enjoy your stay on the Valley Isle and *mahalo* for flying Aloha Airlines. Aloha."

Paula and Christy grabbed their purses.

"That was sure a quick flight! My hair is a mess!" Paula gasped.

"Mine too! Do you have a mirror?"

"Here, help yourself." Paula opened her purse and offered its contents to Christy.

The two girls quickly combed, spritzed and squirted their hair in an effort to be presentable.

The plane made a smooth landing, and soon the passengers stood, excitedly squishing into the aisle and moving like cattle toward the front exit. The flight attendant, wearing a flowered muumuu and a gardenia behind her ear, smiled and said her Hawaiian thank-you of *mahalo* to each passenger.

The herd of passengers kept Christy, Paula and Mom boxed in as they moved through a long passageway into the terminal. Christy's gaze swooped back and forth, looking for Todd. She felt almost panicky with anticipation.

Todd! Where are you?

"Stay together now, girls," Mom instructed. "Keep an eye out for Bob. Marti said she'd tell him to wait at the airport for us."

You look for Bob; I'm looking for Todd!

They stepped expectantly through the automatic doors. The only official island greeter was a warm trade wind that gusted on them, destroying their hairdos.

Oh, great! So much for fixing my hair. Did Todd see my hair get whipped just now? Where is he?

Just then Christy felt something tossed over her head from behind and looped around her neck.

"Aloha!" said a warm voice behind her. "You made it!"

It was Uncle Bob, heaping flower leis on them, all delivered with kisses and much commotion. Christy looked behind Bob, then to the side of Mom, then over Paula's head.

Didn't Todd come to meet us? Where is he?

Christy spun all the way around. There he was.

Tall, tan and smiling, Todd leaned against a pillar, hanging back from all the frenzy. He calmly held out to her a fragrant, white-flowered lei. His boyish grin and outstretched arms invited Christy to join him.

With three shy steps, Christy left the circle of Bob's

joyful greetings and entered another circle. A circle that held only her and Todd. He moved closer, calmly smiling, and placed the lei over her head.

After the traditional Hawaiian kiss on the cheek, she heard his golden voice say, "Aloha, *Kilikina!*"

What a dream! Christy thought, fixing her gaze on his brilliant, silver-blue eyes. *What did he call me? Kilikina! What does that mean? Oh, Todd! I wish I could say all the things I'm feeling right now.*

"And there's Todd!" Mom said, bursting into their bubble, releasing the dreamers and bringing all the commotion with her.

Todd immediately responded by taking the next white flowered lei off his arm and placing it around Mom's neck with the same gesture of an aloha kiss.

"This is beautiful! Thank you, Todd. Oh, and Todd, this is Paula. Paula, this is Todd."

What Christy saw that moment terrified her.

Paula absolutely froze in place. She wasn't even blinking. Obviously all Paula saw was Todd. Totally Todd. Nothing else existed in her world at that moment. She wasn't smiling; she wasn't breathing. She was fixed on Todd.

Her words from the plane came rushing over Christy like a wild gale, "If I don't get a boyfriend during this trip . . ."

Not Todd, Paula. No way! Stop looking at him like that!

Bob broke the spell. "So, you caught the next flight with no problem." He said it in his usual carefree, good-natured manner.

Bob looked like he belonged on an island, with his

flower-print shirt, shorts and thongs. Todd had on the same sort of "native" attire. They looked as though they'd been on Maui all their lives, not just a few days.

Todd casually slipped a lei over Paula's head and brushed her cheek with an aloha kiss.

Paula responded by enthusiastically throwing her arms around Todd's neck and returning the kiss to his right cheek.

That does it, Paula! Stay away. Don't you dare touch him again!

"It's really quite a story," Mom said with a laugh.

They'd begun walking toward the parking lot, and Paula slid in right next to Todd, looking up at him like a dreamy-eyed Miss Piggy, gushing over Kermit.

This time the Piggy-Kermie image did not initiate a giggle inside Christy. Instead, every possessive, jealous response Christy had within her sprang into action.

She grabbed Todd's arm and said coyly, "So this is why you said we'd have such a good time! You knew I was coming all along, didn't you? How could you keep this a secret, Todd?"

Paula followed Christy's example by clutching Todd's other arm and declaring in her most exuberant manner, "You've got to teach me how to surf, Todd! Promise me you'll teach me! Okay? Promise? I just have to learn how to surf. That's like my ultimate, all-time dream!"

Poor Todd, Christy thought. *Without warning you've been pounced on by two Miss Piggys. It's up to you, Kermit the Todd. Which one of us is it going to be?*

Bob interrupted before Todd had a chance to respond to

either of the "Piggys." "Marti and David went ahead in the van with all the luggage. The five of us are going to squeeze in the other car we rented. It's only about a forty-five minute drive to the condo."

"We don't mind!" Paula said pertly. "We just can't believe we're finally here! And these flowers!" Paula used her free hand to lift the two leis to breathe in their fragrance.

"What are these?" she asked Todd. "I love them!"

"Plumeria," Todd answered. "The big white and pink ones are plumeria, and the little white ones are tuberose."

"Oh, I love them! They smell so . . . so . . . exotic!" Paula went on, still clinging to Todd.

"You told me about the plumeria before," Christy said, slightly tugging on his arm, hoping for Todd's full attention. "Weren't these the kind of flowers you could smell on the way to school when you lived here?"

"Yeah," Todd said, turning his head to look completely at Christy. "You remember me telling you that?"

Yes, Todd, oh yes! I remember everything you tell me. Ignore her; look at me! I'm the one who's been listening to you for more than a year. Don't let Paula come between us.

Bob stopped in front of a red Jeep and said, "Tight squeeze. What do you think? Will you three be okay in the back?"

Paula broke into one of her squealing sessions and scrambled into the backseat. "A Jeep! I'm so sure! I've always wanted to ride in a Jeep! And a red one too! I'm not kidding! This is, like, one of my all-time, biggest dreams! Can you believe this? Come on, you guys, let's hit it!"

She stood up in the middle of the backseat and held on to

the roll bar, acting like she was in some kind of dune-buggy race. The wild wind had totally destroyed their hair when they came out of the terminal, and now Paula's short ends stuck up even more dramatically.

Bob helped Mom into the front seat, and Paula positioned herself snugly in the middle of the backseat. Christy stood her ground in the parking lot, fuming that Paula would try to pull off this seating maneuver, guaranteeing she'd sit next to Todd.

Todd began to climb into the backseat when Uncle Bob said, "You know, it's just a suggestion, but you kids might consider letting the person with the longest legs sit in the middle. Like I said, it's a tight squeeze, and long legs can fall asleep back there awfully quick."

Paula slid to the side behind the driver's seat and said, "You win, Todd! You have the longest legs." Then she patted the seat, indicating right where he should sit.

Todd obliged. Christy made a less than graceful entrance and wondered how Paula managed to "gazelle" her way in so easily.

Bob was right. It was a tight squeeze, and Christy, being the last one in, found she only had enough room to sit on one hip, with her long legs crossed and tangled together. Mom fortunately was able to scoot her seat forward, allowing Christy a few more inches of wiggle space.

Paula chattered on, holding Todd's attention while Bob put the Jeep in gear and hummed through the parking lot, down the narrow streets, past the airport and out of town.

The adventure of riding in the Jeep in the warm air thrilled Christy until they were out of town. Then Bob picked up speed and zipped past the sugarcane fields. Christy's hair whipped her face mercilessly. It became impossible to hear anyone talking, except Paula, who had no difficulty yelling her sentences of excitement.

She asked Todd what everything was as they passed it, and Todd was gracious enough to answer once for Paula, then lean forward and give the same explanation to Mom and Christy. He pointed out the pineapple fields; an old sugarcane mill; and the cloud-covered top of Haleakala, a ten-thousand-foot volcanic crater.

When they could see the ocean, he pointed out the neighboring islands of Molokini and Kahoolawe and then the pineapple island, Lanai, when it came into view.

They entered a short tunnel, dug through the black volcanic rock, and for one wonderful moment the wind couldn't tease Christy's hair. She pulled all the tiny strands out of her eyes and mouth. Paula, of course, didn't have that problem with her new, short haircut.

The ride was annoying but not terrible. Being in the Jeep and next to Todd was a wonderful feeling in itself. Christy felt relieved, though, when they stopped at a red light in the first real town they came to and Bob said, "Our condo is about ten miles up the road. You guys going to make it?"

"Sure!" Paula answered for all of them.

Todd leaned over and told Christy, "This is Lahaina."

"Is this where you lived?" Christy asked.

"Yeah, when I was a kid. It's a great old town. A lot of history. A hundred-fifty years ago the whalers and sailors used to spend their winters here. But before the Westerners came, when it was unspoiled, the Hawaiian royalty lived here—surfed here too."

"Really?" Christy asked. "Have you ever surfed in the same spot?"

Todd nodded. "My friend Kimo and I used to go there after school, and all the older guys would make fun of us because Kimo used a long board that belonged to his dad. Funky, old, wooden thing. Then one day this guy came to the beach and offered Kimo big bucks for the board to put it on display in some museum."

"I bet the older guys stopped laughing then!" Christy said.

The light turned green, and they were on the move again, with the wind scattering Todd's answer. The wind, however, did not scatter his expression. He looked directly at her and smiled a real, honest, Todd-smile that showed his dimple. He'd been resting both his arms across the backseat for some time, but now he put his right hand on her shoulder and gave it a squeeze.

Christy returned the warm smile, wishing she could completely relax and disconnect all her jealous, competitive feelings. She felt self-conscious about how her windblown hair must look. She also felt uncomfortably aware that when Todd squeezed her shoulder, as romantic as that was, his arm crushed all the beautiful flowers on the back part of her lei.

Come on, Christy! Lighten up! You're in Maui. Why are you worried about squished flowers and messed-up hair? He just squeezed your shoulder, not Paula's. He's glad you're here!

Paula didn't appear to feel self-conscious about anything, as she eagerly pointed and said, "That's more sugarcane, right?"

Todd nodded and talked directly to Paula, pointing out something on her side of the Jeep. Bob kept driving past condominium complexes until they finally pulled into an underground parking lot and parked the Jeep next to a light blue minivan.

The squeals of delight and excitement started all over again as they tumbled into the elevator and joked about their windswept hair. Even Todd's short, sandy-blond hair looked ruffled.

Bob's two condos, located on the sixth floor, both had their front doors open, and the balmy sounds of Hawaiian music floated from one of the stereos.

"You made it!" Marti said when they converged on her. She looked startled. "We've only been here a few minutes it seems. David went on down to the pool, and I was about to call all the airlines to see which flight you were coming in on."

It took Marti only a minute to gain her composure before starting in on room assignments. Christy and Paula were given the guest bedroom to share, and Mom had the master bedroom in that same unit. Todd and David shared the guest bedroom in the condo next door, and Bob and Marti, of course, had that master bedroom.

"Point me toward my luggage," Paula said. "I want to change and hit the beach!"

Marti pointed, and Paula called over her shoulder, "Oh, Mr. Surf Instructor? Are you ready for my first lesson?"

"The big kahuna surf instructor," Bob intercepted, "is on

wallpaper duty this afternoon, I'm afraid. You girls go on down to the pool. It should only take us another two or three hours to get the wallpaper up in the bathroom."

"Yeah," Todd said good-naturedly, "two or three Hawaiian hours."

"What's that?" Christy asked.

"You'll find out. People around here are on 'island time.' Two or three hours Hawaiian time usually turns out to be half a day mainland time."

With a smile to Christy he added, "The big kahuna boss says I can have tomorrow off if I work real hard today. You want to see what we've done so far?"

Christy followed Todd around the condo, admiring the freshly painted walls and listening patiently to him explain how tricky it was to peel off the three layers of wallpaper in the hallway. Todd obviously took real pride in his work, and that was fun for her to see.

When he went back to work with Bob, Christy stepped into the living room. She could hear Paula's laughter bubbling up from the pool below, where she and David had begun a splash war. Mom and Marti stood on the front balcony, or *lanai*, as Marti called it, looking past Paula and David in the pool and admiring the turquoise blue Pacific.

Christy joined them, breathing in the moist, tropical air and noticing the perfectly clear, blue sky. Everything looked exactly like she thought Hawaii would—tall palm trees swaying in the breeze; caramel-colored sand kissed endlessly by gentle, white-laced waves; lounge chairs around a sparkling swimming pool; and Paula swimming in her new, hot pink bikini.

Paula swimming in her new, hot pink bikini!

Christy's first instinct was a "sisterly" one—she'd tattle. "Mom," she began, very determined. "I need to talk to you about a few things."

"Yes?" Mom looked surprised. Probably because Christy usually didn't come across so forcefully.

"Would you like me to leave?" Marti asked.

"No, it's something you both need to know. It's about Paula."

Mom and Marti gave Christy their full attention.

"First of all, I found her one-piece bathing suit in the dirty clothes last night. I put it in my suitcase, because I didn't know if she forgot it or if maybe she was trying not to bring it."

"But I paid for her new one." Marti looked over the edge of the lanai. "She's wearing the new one; so what's the problem?"

Christy looked to Mom for backup.

Mom explained that she'd talked to Paula about wearing the one-piece for swimming, especially around the guys. "I think her mother would want her to dress a little more modestly than the pink bathing suit."

Marti laughed and looked at Mom as if she couldn't believe her own sister could be so prudish. "Around the guys? For goodness sakes! That's David down there swimming with her! David barely knows the difference between boys and girls yet. Certainly she doesn't need to wear a one-piece for David's sake!"

Mom didn't answer.

Christy tried to reason with her aunt. "It doesn't matter if it's David or, or . . . Kermit the Frog! The point is she said she'd wear the one-piece when she went swimming, and then she left it at my house. I think she did it on purpose, because she didn't even miss it when she got here and changed to go swimming. She just put on the pink one, and now she's swimming in it."

Marti gave Christy another look that made Christy feel like a miserable little snitch. "She looks perfectly modest to me," Marti stated. "I think you're being childish, Christina. Could it be that you are jealous of Paula's lovely figure?"

Christy ignored the question and kept going, realizing she wouldn't get anywhere with Marti on the bathing-suit issue and not at all desiring to be openly compared with Paula in any area.

"Never mind the bathing suit, then. The main thing I wanted to talk to you both about was what happened at the airport. We weren't exactly chased by anyone. Paula thought she saw some movie star, and we started to follow him and got lost. It was all our fault."

Christy felt better for telling what really happened. What confused her was Mom and Marti's response.

Mom shrugged her shoulders. "I don't know what to say, Christy. Everything worked out. I actually think the problem was Marti letting you go on your own in the first place."

"They were only going to get gum," Marti snapped back at Mom. "I believed they were old enough and responsible enough to do that!"

"At an airport, Martha? Didn't you think it would be slightly risky and that they might get lost?" Mom looked mad, not at Christy, but at her sister.

Marti retaliated, "If you hadn't been so late getting us to the airport, none of this would've happened! We would've had plenty of time. So don't try to blame me that you were late!"

A strange, choking pause followed. Mom retreated, putting up her hands in silent surrender. Christy wondered how many times over the years her mom had been the one to back down from her determined sister.

"Christy," Marti said in a sugary, controlled voice, "it would appear to me you're experiencing some sort of sisterly jealousy here with Paula. This is to be expected. After all, you two grew up together. You've been apart for a long time, and now it would be easy for you to be critical of her for many things just because she's different from you. But that's not fair to Paula, now is it?"

Are you talking about Paula and me, or you and my mother? Christy gave a slight nod, which she knew Marti was waiting for.

"Now." Marti put her shoulders back and stuck out her chin. "We are in paradise, and I suggest we all put the past behind us and concentrate on having a wonderful week together."

With a wide smile and an air of confidence that made Christy wince, Marti turned to Mom and said, "Margaret? Why don't we get ourselves something to drink? A diet

Coke? Christy, you really should go on down to the pool and have some fun."

Christy watched as her mom dutifully followed Marti into the kitchen, leaving her alone on the lanai. Her wad of angry thoughts stuck to the inside of her stomach like a pack of chewed bubble gum.

You don't understand! This is serious! Paula is telling lies and getting away with it. She wants a boyfriend—my boyfriend—and she'll do anything to go home with a "victory" to tell her friends about.

"Aren't you going to join the others at the pool, Christy?" Marti called out in her silvery voice from the kitchen.

Everything inside Christy wanted to shout back, "No! Stop trying to run my life!" She held her tongue and her composure and walked past her mom and aunt without looking at them. Then, stepping out the door and retreating into the condo next door where her things were, Christy flopped onto the couch.

I'm going to show Paula she can't play any of her cutesy games around me! Maybe she can get away with it with everyone else, but I see right through her. And Todd will too!

Jumping up, Christy went straight to her suitcase and yanked out Paula's "forgotten" one-piece bathing suit. She laid it out in the middle of Paula's bed.

Chapter 6

"Sweet" Sixteen?

Where did this come from?" Paula asked in an accusing tone, pointing at her old bathing suit on her bed. She and Christy had just come back from several hours down at the pool.

"Oh, I found it back at my house," Christy answered in her most innocent voice. "I thought maybe you'd forgotten it, so I brought it along for you. Now you'll have a bathing suit to swim in, since you said you were only going to sunbathe in the bikini."

Paula didn't answer with words, but her face said plenty. Christy knew she was fuming.

The rest of the evening, Paula ignored Christy and did her best to amuse and entertain everyone else, especially Todd.

Bob took all of them to dinner at a seafood restaurant that was within walking distance. The air felt as balmy as it had when they arrived in the afternoon. A sweet breeze was blowing that puffed up the short sleeves of Christy's blue shirt. Todd was in front of the group with David, and Christy was stuck in the back with Uncle Bob. Paula ended up in the middle between Mom and Marti, talking and laughing loud enough for all of them to hear.

At the restaurant, Mom, Bob and Marti sat at one table, and Todd, Christy, Paula and David sat at the table next to them.

"Order whatever you want, kids," Bob said over his shoulder.

"I want either macaroni and cheese or a hamburger," David said.

"David, this is a seafood restaurant. You should order fish like everybody else," Christy said.

"I'm not having fish," Paula announced. "I hate fish!"

"You might like the fish here," Todd said, looking over his menu. "They have a great variety, and it's all fresh. You want to try some *opakapaka*? Or how about some *hapu'upu'u?*"

"No, thank you! I have a rule about not eating anything I can't pronounce!" Paula smiled cutely, snapped her menu closed and said, "I'm having the New York steak, medium rare, so there."

"How about you, Christy?" Todd asked.

He was sitting next to her, and she'd accidently bumped his knee twice already. Now that he was looking at her, she could feel herself blushing. Or was the heat on her cheeks coming from a tiny bit of sunburn?

"What was that first one you said?" she asked him.

"*Opakapaka.*" Then leaning closer he said, "Don't tell Paula, but it's snapper and *hapu'upu'u* is bass."

He smiled, and Christy smiled back. Not being much of a fish-eater normally, even hearing their names in English, she wasn't sure if she knew the difference between how snapper and bass tasted.

"Have you decided?" The waiter suddenly stood before them. Christy needed more time, but everyone else was ready. She hated these moments when she had to make a quick decision, especially when she barely even knew what she was deciding between.

David ordered a hamburger, Paula ordered steak, and Todd ordered something called *mahimahi* broiled with pineapple rings. Now it was up to her.

"I guess I'll have the New York steak also. Medium well, please." Christy folded her menu and handed it to the waiter.

"See?" Paula mocked. "You knew I was right all along, didn't you, Christy? Never order something you can't pronounce."

Paula's words hit Christy like a bitter slap. Here was yet another area in which Paula seemed to say, "I'm right, and you're wrong."

Todd's comment didn't help much either. "I can see you three aren't exactly ready to live adventurously. I'll have to teach you how to hang loose and live *'da kine* island-style."

"I can be adventurous, Todd, really!" Paula said. "You'll just have to teach me how."

Todd isn't going to teach you a thing, if I can help it! You stay away from him, Paula!

"I'm not sure you can teach anyone to be adventurous. Either you are, or you aren't. I don't think it's a learned thing," Todd said, looking serious. "And living *'da kine* island-style is, well, it's something you just do. You can't teach somebody how to relax."

"Why do you say that '*da* . . . what is it?" David asked.

" '*Da kine*," Todd told him. "It's the pidgin way for saying, 'the kind,' and in Hawaii they use it to mean, well . . . just about anything."

"What's pidgin?" David asked.

"Slang. You know, like an easygoing way of talking. I think pidgin is a combination of all the languages that came to Hawaii. It's the way all my friends and I talked when I was growing up here. Not in school. Just with each other when we were hanging out."

"Like your own secret code?" David asked.

"It's more than that. When you talk pidgin and understand it, it's a way to show other locals you live here and you're not some *malihini*, some tourist, just passing through."

The waiter appeared with four carefully balanced platters on his arm. Christy's steak turned out to be much more than "medium well." Burnt would be more like it. She ate about six bites and gave up when her jaw started to hurt from all the tough chewing.

Todd's fish looked incredible, a large serving of tender, white fish with pineapple rings on top. Christy wished she'd ordered the same.

Next time I'm going to learn from what Todd does. If Paula can have a rule about not ordering anything she can't pronounce, then I can have a rule too. Whatever it says over the restaurant's door, that's what I'll order. If it says "steak house," I'll order steak. But if it says "seafood," from now on, I'll order fish!

David wanted dessert, but Mom said no since he hadn't

finished all his hamburger. Christy didn't want anything but a nice, soft bed. It had been a full day, and they were all too exhausted to even watch TV after they walked back to the condo.

Without saying much to each other, Christy and Paula both soon floated off to sleep, lulled by the endless rocking of the ocean right outside their window.

It seemed to Christy she'd only been asleep for an hour when she slowly opened her eyes and surveyed the surroundings of the bedroom in the brightness of the morning light. It took her a moment to realize it was morning already, and this wasn't part of the sweet dream she'd been in all night.

This was a real dream. A waking dream with a real ocean outside her open window and calm morning breezes tiptoeing across her face.

We're in Hawaii, and today is . . . hey! Today's my birthday!

"Paula," she whispered to the lump of sheets on the bed across the room, "Paula, wake up!"

Paula wasn't in the bed, and she wasn't in the bathroom either. Tumbling into a pair of shorts and a T-shirt, Christy quietly checked in Mom's room. Empty too.

"They must all be next door," she decided while washing her face and doing a few twists with the mascara wand on her eyelashes. She smiled at herself in the mirror. "Maybe it's like a surprise birthday breakfast."

That thought prompted her to plug in her curling iron and pick out a nicer top. She chose a red one. Rick once said he liked her in red.

Rick! I can't believe I thought of Rick. I'm in Hawaii with Todd on my birthday. What am I doing thinking about Rick?

Then she remembered why. For months and months, Rick, a tall, good-looking, popular guy from her school had promised that when she was officially old enough to date, he would take her out. He even told her once that he'd never forget her birthday, July 27, because he'd marked it on his calendar.

Christy set to work curling her hair, reminiscing about the numerous up and down times she'd had with Rick during the school year. She'd never quite figured out if she liked him or not. How convenient, it turned out, that he'd gone to Europe with his family, and she'd gone to Maui. Now the long anticipated and promised birthday date would never take place.

In a way, she felt relieved. Rick, who had just graduated, would go away to college in the fall, and she'd be only an illusive, high-school memory to him. She could pack away her complex bundle of feelings toward him. A nice solution to their "nothing-more-than-friends" relationship.

Putting the curling iron down with a bump, Christy looked in the mirror. She tried to look at herself the same way she'd often looked at Rick. Every time she had, he'd called her "Killer Eyes."

Then, with her chin forward and her voice soft and clear, she said, "Okay, Christy Miller, try explaining this one. If Rick means nothing to you, and you say he never really has, then why is it on your sixteenth birthday, of all the things you could be thinking of, your first thought is of Rick Doyle?

"He is far away, Christy. And he should be far away from your thoughts today. I'm sure he's not thinking of you.

"You're here with Todd, remember? Now go next door and act like you're sweet sixteen, and let Todd, not Rick, make this a birthday to always remember."

After three crisp little knocks on Bob and Marti's door, Christy tried the knob. When she found the door open, she bounced in with a vibrant, "Good morning, everyone!"

Silence. She felt like Goldilocks.

With a much softer voice, she said, "Hello? You guys up yet?"

Oh, how fun! What if they're hiding around the corner, waiting to pop out and surprise me!

Just then the bedroom doorknob turned, and Christy braced herself for the surprise. She was surprised, all right.

Bob, dressed in his pajamas and robe, emerged, yawning like a Papa Bear, so wide that his eyes remained only slits on his groggy face.

"Oh, Christy!" He looked startled to see her. "I didn't see you there. Good morning."

He yawned again. "What got you up so early?"

She followed him into the kitchen. "I thought, I mean, it's, well . . . Paula and Mom were gone, so I thought they were over here."

Bob measured the coffee beans into the grinder, and with a push of a button, the wonderful aroma of ground Kona coffee surrounded them. "Nope. I heard the boys leave more than an hour ago. My guess is Todd went surfing like he has every morning since we got here. I don't know where the rest of them are."

Christy pulled up a stool at the kitchen counter and tried to figure it out. She also tried not to let her hurt feelings show while Bob propped open the front door to let the morning sun and wonderful breeze dance around the room.

"Beautiful day," Bob said, breathing in the morning freshness. "Couldn't ask for a more perfect day."

"Yeah, if you're a weatherman," Christy said under her breath.

Bob turned to look at her. "You hungry?"

"No thanks. I don't feel like eating."

"You want a cup of coffee?"

"No." Then something inside Christy made her change her mind. "Well, yeah, maybe I will. Do you have cream and sugar?"

He handed her everything, and Christy prepared her first cup of coffee. She loved how it smelled but never drank it before because previous sips proved to be so bitter. The cream and sugar would change that. At sixteen years old, she decided, it was time to have her first cup of coffee.

The first taste was awful. She added more cream. That didn't help, so she put in more sugar. By the time she finished her concoction, it tasted like warm hummingbird nectar, and she could only force herself to swallow a few sips.

Bob sliced open a papaya, scooping out the black, pearl-like seeds and squeezing a lime over it. Then he spooned out the orange portion and popped it in his mouth.

"So, tell me," he said. "I haven't heard yet. Did you pass your driver's test?"

"I haven't taken it yet."

"I thought you were going to take it on your birthday?"

Christy felt like sobbing out, "Today is my birthday!"

But before she had a chance, Todd and Paula charged through the open door, laughing and looking like they'd just shared the kind of birthday morning Christy should have been having.

Todd wore a wet bathing suit, and Paula had on her pink bikini with a beach towel wrapped around her waist. Her wet hair gave away that she'd been in the water with Todd. David followed right behind, also wet.

At least David was with them. Knowing that helped, but it didn't diffuse Christy's hurt and anger.

"Christy," Paula gushed, "you should've seen me! I almost got up on the board. A few more tries, and I would've had it. We'll have to try again tomorrow, or maybe later today. You should've come. It was so fun! I love the ocean, and you were right, Christy, the water is really warm."

"I would've loved to come," Christy said flatly, trying to hold back an ocean full of churning emotions.

"I tried to wake you," Paula said, fluffing her hair with her fingers, unaware she was sprinkling little flecks of sand and saltwater across Christy's face.

"You just rolled over and told me to leave you alone, so I did. Face it, Christy. You're a night person. You need to switch over and become a morning person like Todd and me, at least while we're here!" Paula smiled brightly at Todd.

He smiled back and then poured himself a cup of coffee before offering, "She's really good, Christy. You should've seen her. She's got a natural sense of balance."

And I'm a klutz. Go ahead and say it, Todd. You could barely get me to balance on a boogie board last summer. I definitely don't have a natural sense of balance. Go ahead! Tell everyone how uncoordinated I am and how graceful Paula is!

"We came back because the guys were starving," Paula explained. "Todd said he'd take us snorkeling to a place where we can actually feed the fish. He said they like frozen peas. Isn't that wild?"

She bubbled on with a glowing expression that infuriated Christy. "I'm up for the adventure. Are you?"

Then Christy remembered Todd's comments from the restaurant the night before about her and Paula not being adventurous. Now she could see Paula's game. Paula was trying to prove to Todd she already was adventurous, and Christy was a prissy little cream puff.

"I'm so excited! This is going to be so much fun! Todd said he knows a place where we can rent masks and snorkels. We'll get one for you, if you want to go snorkeling too, Christy. Do you? Do you want to come with us?"

"No! I don't want to go on a snorkeling adventure!" Christy spouted loud and sarcastic. "I'd rather stay here all by myself and spend my *birthday* alone in my room!"

Everyone became silent and stared at her.

The intensity, the embarrassment, the anger of the moment, pushed Christy out of her chair, swiftly through the open door and into her condo.

"Christy?" Mom called out as Christy ran past her and

into her room.

"Christy?" Mom followed and stood next to the bed where Christy had thrown herself down face first. "What happened? I went for a walk along the beach, and when I came back, you were gone. What's wrong?"

"Me," Christy sobbed. "I'm wrong. Everything about me is wrong. Why am I such a jerk?"

Mom sat down on the bed and placed a loving hand on Christy's back. "This isn't like you, Christy. What happened?"

Christy didn't answer.

"Is it something with Paula?" Mom ventured.

"Which Paula?" Christy asked between sniffs. "The one I used to know or the new, improved, Adventure Woman, who has Todd wrapped around her little finger?"

"So that's it," Mom said, removing her hand. "Listen, Christy. It's never worth losing a best friend over a guy. And it's silly for you to be jealous of Paula. Actually, I'm kind of surprised. I've always been proud of the nice, healthy relationship you have with Todd."

"Well, what if Todd wants a 'nice, healthy relationship' with Paula instead of me?"

"He might. And that's okay," Mom said calmly.

Christy turned to face her. "No, it's not! You don't understand. Paula wants a boyfriend really bad, and she's setting a trap for Todd."

"Christy, I think you're exaggerating."

"I'm not, Mom. You don't understand." Christy scrambled her thoughts together, trying to figure out how to explain everything she knew to Mom.

It wouldn't matter, though. It hadn't mattered when she told her about the bathing suit or chasing the movie star at the airport. Christy could tell by the kind smile smeared across Mom's face that, regardless of what she said now, it wouldn't matter.

"Christy, let me give you some advice my mother gave me when I was a little bit older than you." Mom paused, then precisely formed her words. "If it is meant for you and Todd to be together, then nothing or no one will be able to break you up. If you're not meant to be together, then nothing you try will keep you together."

Christy rolled Mom's words over in her mind before asking, "Did Grandma say that about you and Dad when you two were dating?"

"No, actually, it was when I was crying over a boy I liked very much. His name was Chuck Clawson."

"What happened to him?" Christy propped herself up on her elbow, intrigued because Mom seldom shared this kind of story.

"Well, as it turned out, he married my best friend, Pat."

"Oh, great!" Christy flopped back on her pillow. "You're supposed to cheer me up, Mother."

Mom looked as if she had expected Christy to be enthusiastic about her story. "Don't you see? God had someone better for me, and that was your father. I didn't know that at the time, because I hadn't met your father. All I knew was how much I liked Chuck and how much I wanted him to like me."

Releasing a deep sigh, Christy said, "It's hard, Mom. It's

really hard."

"Yes, it is hard. So don't make it any harder, okay?"

After a moment Christy pulled herself up and said, "Okay; I'll try. I guess I'd better go apologize to everyone."

"I'll go with you. I want to see if Bob has any more coffee. I can smell it from here."

"I want to apologize to everybody," Christy announced to the group, which was seated around the patio table, chowing down scrambled eggs and toast. "I didn't mean to act like that."

"Don't worry about it!" Paula said, moving her chair closer to Todd to make room for Christy. "If everybody forgot my birthday, I would've thrown a bigger fit than that!"

"Happy birthday, Christy," Bob said, kissing her on the cheek. "Have a seat, and let's try to start this beautiful morning all over again. It'll be a happy birthday, I promise. Ready for some eggs?"

"Sure. They look great," she said, pulling up a chair and listening as they discussed their plans for the day.

More than once Todd caught Christy's eye and looked as though he were trying to ask her something or tell her something. She wasn't sure which. Even though it perplexed her, it made her feel closer to him and gave her hope he really wanted to continue his "nice, healthy relationship" with her and not start something with Paula.

She didn't have a chance to talk to him alone until later that afternoon. All seven of them piled into the van and went snorkeling at a beach Todd called "Black Rock," named for the lava flow of black rock that protruded out into the water.

Black Rock was high enough and the water deep enough that many high-diving tourists followed the supposed old Hawaiian custom of jumping from the rock into the warm water below. Todd jumped three or four times for their cameras and tried to convince David to go off with him. But once David climbed to the top of the rock and found it looked too scary to jump, he took the rocky trail back to the beach.

Christy loved snorkeling. She released handfuls of bright green peas into the water, then watched the fish swim quickly to gobble them up. The colors of the fish amazed her.

Later she stretched out on an air mattress, floating on the calm water above the fish. Todd suddenly popped his head out of the water right by her raft.

"Did you see those little yellow ones?" he asked, lifting his mask up to his forehead.

"I like the ones with the blue and yellow. They look almost iridescent underwater," Christy said.

Todd agreed and then, in his usual, right-to-the-point manner, said, "What was going on this morning?"

"What do you mean?"

"You let it sound like you were upset about your birthday, but something else was bothering you."

"No, nothing was."

"Christy," Todd rested his arms on the raft's side. "You're a bad liar. Your eyes give you away."

She leaned her head back and closed her eyes, her face lifted toward the sun. "I was just tired, that's all."

"Oh, right!" Todd said, and the next thing Christy knew, he had tipped the raft and dumped her into the water.

She came up laughing and splashing as Todd tried to capture the raft.

"Oh no, you don't!" she said, trying her best to flip him over but not succeeding.

They both laughed and splashed each other, and then Christy dove under the raft and tried pulling it out from under him. Todd reached under and grabbed her wrist, pulling her up out of the water.

"Okay, okay, we'll share." Todd slipped into the water up to his waist, resting his elbows on the raft. Christy did the same on the other side of the raft.

Todd didn't use any words. He spoke only with his eyes. Christy knew what he was asking, and she knew she couldn't lie.

"Okay, Paula's bothering me. She's changed so much since we were friends back in Wisconsin."

"So have you."

"Yeah, but I changed for the good when I became a Christian last summer. I know that sounds egotistical, and I don't mean that I'm all perfect now or anything."

Todd smiled.

Christy could guess what he was thinking and added, "I guess I proved that this morning, didn't I?"

"None of us is perfect, Christy."

"Right, but the thing about Paula is she's not even trying to live morally or anything. I wish she'd become a Christian. I'm worried she'll turn out like Alissa."

"Turn out like Alissa? Alissa's not done yet."

"What do you mean?"

"Well, Shawn, for instance. Now, he's done. He doesn't have any more choices or any more chances. He's dead."

It sounded so blunt. Christy winced inwardly and waited for Todd to continue.

"You know, I prayed for Shawn everyday for more than a year. As far as I know, he died without ever surrendering to Christ. And now . . . ," Todd looked away as he spoke. " . . . he's done. They have a word for it in Hawaiian: *pau.*"

"*Pow*?" Christy repeated.

"Yeah, *pau.* Means 'finished,' 'complete,' 'no more chances.' Shawn is *pau.* But Alissa's not. And neither is Paula."

Christy fluttered her legs in the warm ocean water and felt the sun pounding on her back. She thought she understood what Todd was saying.

"I've been praying for Alissa," Todd continued. "Everyday."

"And you think that's what I should be doing with Paula? Praying for her?"

Todd nodded, his smile returning. "And love her for who she is, not for who you want her to be."

"That's hard to do, Todd. I want her to become a Christian so bad."

"That's good. I want her to become a Christian too. You know, it's really God's kindness that leads us to repentance, not his judgment. We have to start praying, *Kilikina.*"

Christy recognized that name as the same one Todd had used at the airport. "What does that word mean?"

"*Kilikina*? That's your name in Hawaiian. Actually, it's

Hawaiian for 'Christina.' 'Christy' would be *Kiliki*."

The word sounded like a wild bird call with the syllables rolling off Todd's tongue. Christy loved the way he said it.

"Say it again."

"*Kilikina*."

"How did you know it?"'

Todd looked down, almost as if he were embarrassed to give her his answer. Without looking up he said, "When I was in the third grade here there was a *haole* girl—"

Christy interrupted, "What's a *how-lee*?"

"A white person. You know, blond, fair-skinned, blue-eyed. Someone who's obviously not Polynesian. Only four of us haoles were in my third-grade class—me, two other guys and then this girl named Christina."

Todd looked at Christy and smiled a third-grader kind of smile. "I had an awful crush on her," he admitted. "The teacher called us all by our Hawaiian names in class, and *Kilikina* was the first name I learned."

Christy thought Todd looked cute, the sun lighting up his hair, elbows propped up on the raft, confessing his first crush to her.

"What's your name in Hawaiian?" Christy asked.

He hesitated, then smiled and said, "*Koka*."

"*Koka*?"

"Yeah, I hated it because all the kids called me *Koka* Cola."

Christy laughed and noticed someone on the shore waving to them. "Is that my uncle?"

Todd looked across the bright glare on the water. "Looks like he wants us to come up. Come on. I'll give you a ride."

Their time together ended too soon for Christy. Every time she talked to Todd she felt as though she learned something new about him, and they became closer to each other.

When she slid all the way onto the raft and stretched out on her stomach, she took in a sweeping view of the clear, sparkling lagoon, the curving shoreline dotted with tourists and, behind the hotels, the smooth, green West Maui Mountains wearing their afternoon halo of baby's-breath clouds.

I will always remember this day, forever. I never would have guessed I'd spend my sixteenth birthday on a tropical island with Todd. Somebody pinch me; I must be dreaming!

She didn't need to be pinched. At that very moment, Todd toppled the raft, and the dousing proved to be sufficient evidence she was awake. They splashed each other some more before Christy resumed her position on top of the raft, then holding tightly, she called, "Take me to shore, mister, and no more funny stuff!"

He looked like a sea turtle, sticking his neck out of the water at intervals while tug-boating her raft back to shore. Christy laughed aloud with glee, wondering how she could have been so angry this morning or why she ever felt Paula could possibly come between her and Todd.

"Marti and your mom already headed for the car," Bob told them when they arrived back at the beach towels, breathless and sparkling with salt water. "David's over there by the tide pools trying to catch a fish, and Paula is about twenty yards down the beach talking to some guys. We need to get going."

"What are we doing for dinner?" Christy asked.

"That's our little surprise," Bob said with a wink. "Why don't you go find Paula? Todd, you get David, okay?"

Christy jogged off down the beach and found Paula sitting on a grass mat next to two guys. By the looks of things, they enjoyed her entertaining conversation. Paula introduced them as Jackson and Jonathan, two members of a band called Teralon.

"We need to get going," Christy said politely. "It was nice to meet you both."

"We're going to a luau tonight," Paula explained. Then she immediately pressed her hand over her mouth, her baby-doll eyes opening wide, and cutely added, "Oops. You didn't hear that, Christy."

"You're in trouble now, Paula," one of the guys teased from behind his dark sunglasses.

"I'd better go," she said, rising to her feet. "Maybe I'll see you guys again."

"You never know," the other guy said as Christy and Paula walked away. "If not here, then hopefully in heaven!"

"Were they Christians?" Christy asked, looking back over her shoulder and returning their friendly wave.

"Slightly!" Paula said. "Of all the guys on the beach, I have to pick two Jesus freaks to talk to. They really were sweet, but all they wanted to talk about was 'the Lord.' "

Paula shook her head. "First Todd this morning with all his bits of spiritual wisdom and now these guys. What's going on here?"

Christy broke into a wide grin, using all her self-control to keep from laughing aloud.

Paula saw the grin, though, and asked, "What? What?"

Christy didn't say a word. She didn't have to. Paula came to the same conclusion Christy had and voiced it with an air of disgust.

"Don't you dare try to tell me meeting those guys was one of your little God-things!"

"Okay, Paula." Christy kept grinning. "I won't tell you."

Chapter 7

Come On, Christy, Show Us How to Hula!

Go ahead," Todd encouraged. "Try some *poi*. You put two fingers in like this."

Todd stuck his fingers in the small, wooden calabash bowl in the center of the table and quickly drew the sticky, gray substance to his lips.

"It looks too gooey," Paula said, making a face. "What does it taste like?"

Todd licked his lips and stuck his fingers back in the bowl. "Like, um, like *poi*. That's it! It tastes like *poi*. Come on, Christy. The birthday girl can't go to a luau and not eat *poi*."

She bravely dipped a finger in and drew it to her lips. "What is this stuff, anyway?"

"The old Hawaiians ate it. It comes from the root of the taro plant. They pound it to make it mushy like this."

Christy touched the tip of her tongue with the *poi*, which had the color and consistency of wallpaper paste. Paula, sitting directly across from her, watched her reaction.

"It doesn't really have a taste." Christy turned to Todd,

who sat next to her. "Did you eat this stuff all the time you lived here?"

"I've had my share. You get enough down there, Bob?"

Bob, Marti, Mom and David all reached for their bowl of *poi* at the same time. Marti was the first to say, "Here, Todd. You can have the rest of ours."

They all laughed, and the merry mood continued through the luau. Christy decided to be adventurous and try a few things she didn't normally eat, like mangoes in the fruit salad and shredded pork wrapped up in ti leaves, which Todd called *laulaus.*

Paula, not demonstrating an adventurous spirit, barely ate a thing besides the white rice. Part of Paula's problem was her sunburn.

All day at the beach Christy had obediently smeared her skin with sunscreen, but Paula had refused, saying she tanned easily and never burned. Even Marti's warnings bounced off Paula, who seemed determined to soak up as much Hawaiian sun as possible, parading her white flesh up and down the beach in her pink bikini.

When they dressed for the luau, Christy had covered herself with aloe vera gel, and now in the coolness of the setting sun, she only was a tiny bit sunburned on her back. Paula's flaming red face proved she'd gotten too much sun. Even her lips and eyelids had swollen. She was hurting, even though she'd convinced all of them on the way to the luau that her stomach felt a little pink, but that was all.

Todd looked incredibly good in his blue-flowered Hawaiian shirt. *Like an island boy*, Christy thought, with his tan face, sun-streaked blonde hair and his screaming silver-blue eyes.

Christy wasn't the only one who noticed how good Todd looked. Paula had once again locked her gaze on Todd, and all during dinner, every time Christy looked up, she felt something was going on between the two of them.

By the time the show began and the Polynesian dancers appeared on stage in their ceremonial costumes, Christy had convinced herself that whatever game Paula was playing, Christy could play it too.

They applauded the talented hula dancers, and when David's favorite, the fire dancer, jumped on the stage, Christy moved her chair closer to Todd for a better view. She slightly moved her arm so that she brushed up against the sleeve of Todd's shirt. She couldn't tell if he noticed or not. He seemed completely caught up in the show.

The show's host came to the microphone and asked for the crowd to "put your hands together" for the fire dancer one more time. Then he asked if there were any birthdays or anniversaries in the group.

David pointed at Christy, whistling loudly. She shrunk down in her seat and prayed they wouldn't make her stand up or anything. To her relief, all they did was ask the group to sing "Happy Birthday" to the six birthday people. It was kind of fun, being sung to, as long as she didn't have to stand. Not too embarrassing.

"You got off easy," Todd said, leaning closer to her. "I thought they were going to call you up on stage."

He barely finished speaking before several guys, dressed in only a cloth around their waists and a wreath of thin, green leaves around their heads, came running through the audience to select their dance partners. One of the brown-skinned dancers appeared at their table and beckoned to Christy, holding out his hand as the drums on the stage beat their commands, "Come, come, come, come . . ."

Christy resisted, sinking into her chair, shaking her head. She could feel her pulse begin to beat time with the drums.

"Go on, Christy," Paula urged. "Go with him!"

"No, you go, Paula. Take her!" Christy suggested, pointing across the table. *Now's your chance to be as adventurous as you want, Paula!*

"Take both *wahines*!" Todd shouted to the dancer. "Make both girls go."

The dancer stood firm, one arm stretched out to Christy and the other arm now pointing to Paula. In a voice much larger than himself, he spoke, "Both *wahines* come!"

And so they did.

The drums changed into Tahitian dance music the minute Christy and Paula stepped onto the stage. They joined the seven other "victims," and in front of more than one hundred people, Christy swayed and wiggled and stamped her feet, feeling silly and embarrassed.

The flowered lei around her neck swished back and forth across her favorite Laura Ashley sundress, and she couldn't tell at all if she looked cute or ridiculous. By the time she'd come up with some kind of pattern for her feet to follow, she had the feeling she looked more like a cheerleader in slow motion than a fluid-moving hula dancer.

Paula was into the dance, wiggling her hips so her white shorts swished back and forth. She locked her blue-eyed gaze on her native dance partner, who by now had turned his back on Christy, totally ignoring her, and was having fun showing off with Paula.

The drums came to an abrupt halt, and the dancer slipped his arm around Paula's waist and said something Christy couldn't hear. She wasn't about to stick around on stage to see if anyone had any secret messages for her.

Quickly making her way down the stage steps, she was aware some people she passed had video cameras. They might have actually taped her embarrassing moment on stage.

Good thing I didn't do anything really embarrassing. I could have ended up on that TV show as one of "America's funniest."

Before she managed to get back in her seat, the girl dancers had spread out in the audience. It didn't surprise Christy to see Todd was one of their first selections. He slid past Christy, shrugging his shoulders and obediently following the *wahine* in the grass skirt.

David laughed at Christy when she sat down, but Bob, Mom and Marti had sweet things to say. They repeated the same bits of praise to Paula when she returned to her seat.

Now it was Todd's turn. The drums began slowly, and the dancers swished their grass skirts back and forth, inviting the guys to follow their motions. Since Todd had proved to be so familiar with Hawaiian ways, Christy sat back, waiting for him to wow the audience with his expert hula dancing.

To her surprise and everyone else's humor, Todd turned out to be a total hula klutz.

"Guys just can't move their hips like that," Paula said in between bursts of laughter. "Look at him! He's the star of the show."

Of the eight or nine men they'd called up on stage, Todd stood out as the worst dancer. A large man in the front row balanced his video camera on his shoulder and taped the whole thing. The funniest part was Todd seemed to be sincerely trying to hula and didn't realize how hilarious he looked with his arms in the air and hips doing a sort of offbeat wiggle.

Before the music ended, all the hula-dancer girls formed a circle with Todd in the middle. They danced around him so all Christy could clearly see were his arms waving in the air.

"I'd try to hide that kind of dancing too," Bob chuckled. "A surfer he is; a dancer he's not."

Bob teased Todd when he sat down by patting him on the shoulder and saying, "We all have our strengths and weaknesses, son. Stick to surfing!"

Christy laughed along with the rest of them, yet she wondered if their teasing hurt Todd's feelings. If it did, he didn't show it. He even made some jokes about himself as they left the luau and began a leisurely stroll along the winding, Kaanapali Beach walkway.

Christy made sure she was positioned right by Todd's side while they walked, wondering if she should clutch his arm the way she did at the airport or wait to see if he'd reach for her hand. At the luau Todd had divided his attention equally between Christy and Paula. Now, with the ocean singing its eternal song only a few yards to their left and the velvet sky sprinkled with diamonds high above them, Christy felt hopelessly romantic.

It's my birthday, Todd. It's my sixteenth birthday, and here we are, walking along the beach in Maui. You have to hold my hand or pay some kind of special attention to me. You have to!

"Todd," Paula chirped loudly, "wait up!"

She left the clump of Bob, Marti, Mom and David and scooted up to Todd's other side, freely clutching his arm and holding it with both hands.

"We should make a deal. You teach me to surf, and I'll teach you to dance. Wouldn't that be fun?"

Christy's mind whirled through a split-second debate on how she could respond to this situation. She could grab Todd's other arm, she could fall back with the grown-ups to test Todd and see if he came back for her, or she could turn into a cat-woman and scratch Paula's eyes out.

Before she could choose the best option, Marti nosed into their threesome and stated, "Paula, I've been wanting a chance to talk with you, and this is the perfect opportunity."

Marti abruptly linked her arm through Paula's and pulled her away from Todd, positioning herself and Paula several feet in front of Todd and Christy.

All right, Aunt Marti! I take back every mean thing I ever thought about you. You really are on my side!

"I've been meaning to tell you, Paula, dear, that with a few simple pointers, I believe you could lose some of your Midwest flavor and take on a more West-Coast style. First, let's evaluate the way you walk . . ." and on Marti went, conducting her unique style of charm school with a rather willing Paula.

Christy thought of a whole string of things to say to Todd as the gentle evening breeze caressed her shoulders, awakening the sweet fragrance in her plumeria and tuberose leis. But she couldn't get herself to jump in and start talking, because she kept hoping Todd would slip his arm around her or take her hand. When he didn't, she struggled miserably over how she could encourage him, even though Mom, Bob and David were right behind them watching. She knew she was capable of being bubbly and a little bit forward like Paula. She could easily slip her arm through Todd's and say, "Isn't it a gorgeous night? What a perfect setting for my birthday! Isn't it romantic, Todd?"

Okay, Christy, she coached herself. *Go ahead. Make a move. Paula would, if she were you.*

"You know," Todd sliced through the silence between them and leaned close so the others couldn't hear what he said, "that's one of the things I like most about you, Christy. You don't play games or try to be flirty like a lot of other girls."

She swallowed hard, feeling caught.

If only you knew, Todd! One more minute, and I would have been playing "Miss Piggy."

"It's not that I don't think about it," Christy said, shocked that the honest words tumbled out before she could stop them.

"Really?" Todd looked at her curiously. "What do girls think about? I mean, why do they do that to a guy?"

Christy didn't allow herself to hesitate. If she did, she might not say any of the things she truly felt or thought. Things she often wanted to talk over with Todd but usually chickened out on before she said them.

"I guess we're looking for some attention, some way to find out what the guy is thinking or how he feels about us."

"That's all backwards," Todd stated. "I think the guy should be the initiator, and the girl should be the responder. Not the other way around."

"But you don't know what it's like to be the girl and to have to wait and wait and wait for the guy to initiate something. When he doesn't, you feel he's not interested in you."

"So girls think that the level of a guy's interest is based on how much he touches her?" He sounded surprised, and his voice rose a bit.

Christy wondered if everyone else could overhear their conversation. But she was saying so many things to Todd she had longed to tell him that she continued but spoke softly.

"I agree a girl should let the guy be the leader, but I also think sometimes the guy can be a little more, well, gentle and caring by, you know, holding her hand or other little expressions of how he feels without it being a big deal." Christy looked up at Todd, and in the dim light she could see an amazed expression on his face, as if he'd never considered that point of view before.

"Does this make sense?" she asked. "What I'm trying to

say is that if a guy holds a girl's hand or something like that, it lets the girl know he likes her. That's all. It doesn't mean he's trying to, you know, make out with her or anything. It just means she's special to him."

"Interesting. It's different for guys," Todd said. "For a guy it's like—"

He didn't get to finish his sentence, which frustrated Christy, because Bob interrupted them. He directed them to stop at Whalers' Village and find a seat on the patio at Leilani's Restaurant.

David helped Todd push two of the round tables together under the light of a gas tiki torch and pull up seven chairs. David then made a beeline for the seat next to Todd. Then, before Christy could get around to the other side, Paula grabbed the chair on Todd's other side. Feeling like she'd been cut off from one of the best conversations she'd ever had with Todd, Christy dropped into a chair next to Marti.

"Oh, Christy," Marti scolded, "that certainly is not the way a young lady takes her seat! I thought I'd taught you better than that."

Fortunately the waitress stepped up to their table, and Christy didn't have to answer.

"We'll have seven Naughty Hula pies," Bob ordered for them all. "And how many coffees?"

"Bob," Marti interjected, "I only want a little bite of yours, and perhaps the girls would like to split one. The slices are gigantic, and they're awfully rich."

"Not the birthday girl!" Bob said, flashing a warm smile at a pouting Christy. "Tonight she gets whatever she wants."

If that were true, I'd get Todd all to myself, and I'd hold his hand tight, and I'd find a way to tell him how I feel about him. If I could wish for anything on my birthday, that would be it.

They all ordered their own slice of pie, except Marti. Then they laughed at their optimism when the huge slices of macadamia-nut ice-cream pie, covered with hot fudge and whipped cream, arrived at their table.

"I tried to warn you," Marti said. "Now you know why they call it Naughty Hula pie. Can you even begin to guess how many calories are in this monstrous piece?"

"Let's sing to the birthday girl and let her enjoy her pie without the guilt," Bob suggested. "Go ahead, honey. Make a wish."

Christy closed her eyes. She knew exactly what to wish for.

On the drive to the condo, Christy felt overly full, yet not willing to tell her aunt she had been right about the size of the pie. She told herself she'd wasted her birthday wish on something that would never come true. Todd wasn't even sitting by her in the van. He sat by David on the back bench seat, with Paula close on his other side.

"You have something in your hair, Todd," Paula said. Christy turned slightly in her middle seat, so she could see what game Paula was up to now. Paula began to comb her long fingernails through the side of his hair, leaning close in the dark car to find the something in his hair.

"Get it?" Todd asked.

"I'm not sure. It's kind of dark in here." She kept grooming his short, sun-lightened mane. "You really have nice hair, Todd."

Let go of him, Paula! Stop your stupid little games. Todd hates your games, anyway. You're not going to score any points with him this way.

"That feels good," Todd said. "Little more to the left."

He leaned his head closer to her, so she could keep scratching.

"Eww! I think you still have sand in your hair!" Paula squealed.

"Probably. I need fingernails like yours to get it out, I guess."

That's just great, Todd. Now who's playing games?

Christy curled her hands into two fists in her lap. The cat-woman image re-entered her mind, and she wondered if anyone would try to stop her if she sprang from her seat and used her claws on Paula at this very moment.

But they were home.

Bob parked the van, and the sand-scratching ritual in the backseat came to an end.

Scrunched together in the elevator, Christy shot angry darts at Todd. Being mad at Paula was one thing. She expected Paula to play all her games to win Todd's attention, regardless of this being Christy's birthday. But why, oh why, would Todd say he didn't like it when Paula played those games and he liked Christy because she didn't play them, and then give in to Paula whenever she came on to him? Didn't he see what he was doing when he accepted her attention? Didn't he understand how that made Christy feel?

"I'm going to bed," David announced when the elevator

deposited them on the sixth floor. "I don't feel very good."

"We have a few presents for Christy. Can you wait until after she opens them?"

"No," David groaned, holding his stomach, "I'm too full to sit up. I just want to go to bed."

David went right to his room, while the others gathered on Bob and Marti's lanai to admire the stars. While everyone chatted, Christy stared into the vast ocean before her.

She had to admit, the night was beautiful. She didn't want to ruin what was left of her birthday with such a bitter attitude.

I'm sorry, Father. She sent her heartfelt prayer on a sudden breeze that rustled the huge palm tree growing beside the lanai. *Please help me not to be so jealous but to act the way You want me to.*

Then she remembered. Today, or more accurately tomorrow, was her spiritual birthday. One year ago she had given her heart to the Lord.

I'm not exactly acting like one of Your daughters, am I, God? I'm sorry.

"You going to join us, Christy?" Marti called from the lanai table. "We have some presents here, and they all have your name on them."

Christy took a breath and allowed a smile to replace her scowl. As demurely as possible, she sat in the seat next to her aunt, secretly pleased with her delicate descent.

The night wasn't over yet. A few dreams could still come true.

Chapter 8

Mystery Call From the Blue Grotto

Open my present first," Paula urged, sitting, of course, right next to Todd. "It was actually my mom's idea. I hope you like it."

Even in the dim light on the lanai, Paula looked horribly sunburned.

"Did you use anything for your sunburn yet?" Marti asked. "You really got too much sun today, Paula. You can get sick from sunburn, you know. Your lips will swell and blister, and your skin will peel. You *did* use sunscreen today, didn't you?"

Paula avoided answering by focusing on Christy, who had opened the small box from Paula and lifted out a picture in a heart-shaped, silver frame. Christy held it closer in the dim light to see better.

"It's us," Paula said. "My mom took it on our first day of kindergarten."

Christy held it up to the light and smiled at the two little faces, pressed cheek to cheek. Both had a front tooth missing.

Christy couldn't explain it, but all of a sudden she felt like crying. The picture delighted her. It warmed her from the inside out. It brought an ocean full of childhood memories and dreams. It made her feel closer to Paula than she had felt their whole trip. She couldn't be angry with that little cherub beside her in the picture.

"I love it, Paula. Thank you." Christy reached over to give her a cheek-to-cheek hug.

"Owww!" Paula responded the instant Christy touched her.

"Oh, I'm sorry. It's your sunburn, huh?"

Instantly the surge of closeness receded. An invisible shield went up between them again.

Mom and Marti admired the picture and handed it to Todd for his examination.

A smile spread across his face, and he teased, "Which is which?"

"Can't you tell?" Christy asked. "I'm the one on the right."

Todd kept looking at the picture and smiling.

Mom handed Christy her gift in a shopping bag and apologized for not being organized enough to have brought along a box and wrapping paper. It was a big, multi-colored, straw beach bag.

Christy really liked it, which was good since she and Mom usually didn't have similar tastes.

"Here," Todd said, pulling a cardboard tube out from under his chair. "I'm not one for wrapping paper either."

Popping the plastic end off the tube, Christy pulled out a rolled up picture of a gorgeous waterfall surrounded by tropical foliage. An old bridge stretched across the top of the waterfall.

"This is pretty. Thanks." It *was* a pretty picture, but it

wasn't exactly a personal, romantic kind of gift like the gold ID bracelet he had given her for Christmas. He had had the word *forever* engraved on it. Christy had grown familiar with its light touch on her wrist and all the hope and promise for their relationship that it carried.

"You said to send you a postcard of a waterfall," Todd said in his teasing way. "And that's a waterfall that, well . . ."

He looked as though he wanted to explain something about the waterfall, but it was too deeply personal. ". . . well, I like it a lot."

Christy smiled her thanks, unsure of his unspoken message, and rolled the picture back up. Gently she eased it into the tube.

"One more gift, Christy," Marti said with a song in her voice.

Christy felt even worse at the thought she might now receive an expensive gift. "You've already given me my birthday present, bringing me here and taking us to the luau and everything! I really couldn't accept anything else."

Bob handed her an envelope, and she felt a bit relieved, thinking it might be a card with twenty dollars or something that would be easy to accept.

It was a card, all right. "Happy sweet sixteen," the front proclaimed. Fortunately no money was inside. Only an odd-shaped piece of paper that floated to her lap. Christy held it up and then looked at her aunt and uncle and asked, "What's this?"

"Can't you tell?" Marti bubbled. "It's a clue. Try to guess."

"It's a picture of a car."

"A car!" Paula spit out the words as if they disgusted her. "I'm so sure, Christy! You're so spoiled, and you don't even know it."

"Hold on now," Bob said calmly. "It's not a brand new car."

"Remember my old car?" Marti asked.

Christy gulped, "The convertible Mercedes?"

Paula turned away and looked out at the ocean.

"We traded it in," Bob explained. "Well, sort of traded it in. The bottom line is, after you get your license, you and your dad will go with me to the dealer and trade in your parents' car as well. We'll use the credit from their car and the Mercedes to do a little wheeling and dealing. Hopefully we can manage to come up with a car for you and one for your mom and dad as well."

"I can't believe this! Thank you." Christy hugged Bob and Marti and then Mom.

Her stomach had begun to do flip-flops the moment Bob said "when you get your license," and now she felt that strange sensation of horror and expectation. So much depended on her taking the test when she got home and passing it the first time.

Just then the phone rang inside the condo.

"Who could that be?" Marti asked. "After all, your father already called this morning."

"Want me to get it?" Christy offered since she was the only one standing.

"Sure," Bob said.

Christy lifted the receiver on the third ring. "Hello?"

A loud crackling and clicking came across the line.

"Hello?" she said louder. "Hello?"

A woman spoke in what sounded like Spanish or Italian, and then the phone clicked and a surprisingly clear male voice came on the line. "Yes, hello. I'm trying to reach Christy Miller."

"This is Christy." Her heart pounded, echoing in her ears. *This is strange! Who could be calling me?*

"Christy! Do you know who this is?" There was a delay and a little bit of an echo, which made it even more difficult to identify the deep, vaguely familiar voice.

"Ah, ahh . . ." She didn't know what to say.

Obviously this person knew her, knew she was in Maui and somehow got the phone number. Suddenly she remembered the mysterious, unsigned letter she had stuck in her purse. Could this be the person who wrote the letter?

The voice laughed on the other end of the line, and she knew she had heard that laugh before. But where? When? Who was this?

"I'll give you a clue. You owe me something, which you promised to give me on July 27. Well, where I'm calling from, it's already July 28, but I'm calling to tell you that just because you're in Maui, you can't forget your promise. You still owe me."

The strong voice had taken on a Mafia-type accent, and Christy felt a little frightened, even though she knew it had to be someone playing a trick on her.

"I intend to collect on what you owe me before the

summer's over, got it?"

"Well, um." Christy tried hard to sound light and playful, but she was in a fog over what this masked voice was talking about. "Just exactly what is it I owe you?"

The voice laughed, not deep and mysterious, but freely, in its natural range. Then switching back to Mafia style, he said, "A date, Killer Eyes. You owe me a birthday date."

Christy burst out in wild, relieved, delighted laughter, causing everyone on the lanai to stop talking and look inside the condo at her. She pulled the phone cord around the corner, into the kitchen to be out of their view.

"Rick! I can't believe you're calling me!"

"You really didn't know it was me?" he asked in his usual, self-confident tone.

"No, I couldn't figure it out at all! Where are you? I thought you were in Europe."

"I am. I'm on the island of Capri."

"Where's that?"

"Off the coast of Italy. We took a hydrofoil over from Naples yesterday. We're going to Rome later this afternoon and then up to Florence and Venice."

"I can't believe this. How'd you get my number?"

"I called your home yesterday. Your dad told me you were in Maui, and he gave me your number. It was easy. You didn't think I'd forget your birthday, did you?"

"But Rick, this is going cost you a fortune!"

"About the same as dinner and a movie in Escondido," he teased. "We'll compare prices when I take you out in August. If we plan it just right, there should be about a week before I leave for college, and we'll celebrate your birthday then. You pick the day."

"Okay." She knew she should keep talking, but her mind went blank. She felt her cheeks burning and heart pounding over Rick calling her all the way from Europe. He hadn't forgotten her birthday. She never expected this.

"I thought of you yesterday," Rick said in a low, rich voice. "We went to the Blue Grotto. You ever heard of it?"

"No."

The overseas phone line echoed her "no" before Rick continued. "We got in this little boat, kind of a cross between a row boat and a gondola. The guy paddled us into this place like a cave, and we had to scrunch down on the bottom of the boat because the opening was so low. Inside, the water is the most unusual color of blue. The sun reflects into the cave somehow. I don't remember what does it, but the whole inside looks blue from the sunlight and the reflection off the water onto the rocks."

"Sounds pretty," Christy said.

"Not just pretty. Incredible. Awesome. Outrageous. It was killer, Christy. Just like your eyes. I felt like the whole cave was filled with Christy."

He paused, and Christy let the romance of his words sink in. "That's where I would've taken you for your birthday if I could've picked anywhere in the whole world, Christina. I would've taken you to the Blue Grotto on this island of Capri."

There was a pause, during which Christy felt certain the sound of her heart pounding in her ears had exploded through the phone and burst in on Rick on the other side of the world.

His voice switched back to teasing, and he said, "We'll have to check out all the Italian restaurants in southern California and see if there's a Blue Grotto restaurant somewhere. If there is, that's where we'll go in August."

Christy laughed. "Okay. Sounds like fun."

"It will be," Rick said confidently. "You try to have a happy birthday there without me, okay? I know it'll be hard, but try."

"Okay. Thanks for calling."

"Did you think for one minute I wouldn't call? That shows how little you know me, Christy. We'll work on improving that in a few weeks. Until then, *ciao!*"

" 'Bye, Rick."

She stood perfectly still for a moment before hanging up the phone.

How bizarre! Why would he call me and say all those sweet, sweet things? I never would have expected that from Rick. Never. Maybe I don't know him, like he said.

Christy started toward the lanai, not sure of how to answer when they all asked who was on the phone. What an unexpected birthday evening! First the car from Bob and Marti, then Rick's call.

Fortunately no one asked about her call right away. They were involved in an argument, and when Christy entered, Marti appeared to have won.

"Do like I said, Paula. Take a lukewarm bath, and put the aloe vera gel all over your sunburn. Do it now, or you're going to be much worse in the morning. Go on!"

Paula slowly stood, showing clearly that every movement caused her pain.

"You want some help?" Christy offered.

"Doing what?" Paula snapped. "Running my bathwater? I think I can handle that myself."

"I just thought—"

Bob cut off Christy. "You holler if you need anything, Paula."

Mom rose and said, "I was going back to our condo anyway. I'll go with you, Paula."

"Whatever you do, don't touch me anywhere!" Paula warned as the two of them exited, followed by Marti.

"I'll get her some extra aloe gel in case the tube in her bathroom is low." Marti set off, Christy thought, to make sure her instructions were followed thoroughly.

"Well," Bob said, pushing himself up from the chair. "I'm ready to call it a day. Can I get you two anything? Something to drink?"

"No thanks."

Just that fast, Christy and Todd were alone on the lanai. Bob had turned on the news on the TV right behind the sliding glass door and stood in front of it rather than sitting down.

Todd stood up and moved his chair over so he would be right next to Christy.

They sat silently for a few minutes, gazing at the ocean and the sky full of stars. The moon sprinkled light on the wave crests. Christy thought it looked as if a giant bottle of silver glitter had spilled from the deep heavens and all the tiny flecks' were now stuck to the waves with frothy, white, Elmer's glue.

Thoughts of Rick evaporated; dreams of Todd soared.

This is so beautiful! What a perfect night, and how romantic to be here with Todd. I love the way he moved his chair over to be next to me. This is exactly what I wished for! I wonder what he's thinking?

"How's Rick?"

"Rick?" Christy echoed.

Todd kept looking straight ahead into the night. "That was Rick, wasn't it?"

"Yes, but how did you know?"

Todd turned and gave her a look that said, "We guys know these things, okay?"

"He's fine. I guess. He's in Italy."

"Italy?"

"His family is on vacation there," she explained.

Is Todd jealous of Rick the way I'm jealous of Paula?

Todd kept looking out at the ocean, his jawline pressed forward like it did when he was deep in thought or about to say something profound.

Christy waited.

Todd remained silent.

Then Christy did something rather bold for her. She knew Bob was still in the living room watching TV right behind them, but this was her birthday. Her sweet sixteenth, and this was her wish—to be alone with Todd. She slipped her hand through Todd's arm, which rested on the chair. Todd immediately responded by reaching for her hand and meshing their fingers together. Christy felt relieved. Calmed. Full of birthday wishes. She hoped that her reaching out to him like this would assure him there was really nothing going on between her and Rick. At least, she didn't think anything was going on between her and Rick.

Todd silently stroked Christy's forever bracelet with his thumb, watching the ocean, studying the darkness without saying anything. Christy thought of about fifty different things to say but kept silent too. She knew she didn't have to apologize for Rick calling, and she knew she didn't have to defend her feelings for anybody.

She wished she could find words from her heart that would tell Todd how she felt for him. Every time she had tried to explain it in the past, she had gotten all goofed up and felt silly. She could write her feelings for him accurately and had many times in her diary. But she didn't know how to say what she felt. Maybe Todd didn't either.

"See Molokai over there?" Todd broke the silence with a quiet yet direct voice.

Christy knew two islands were visible from the condo, Lanai and Molokai. If she remembered correctly, Molokai was to their right.

"Yes," she answered, following Todd's gaze to the right.

"It's less than nine miles away. See those two lights?"

Christy noticed for the first time that on the dark, sparsely populated island two lights twinkled like stars, right next to each other on the shoreline. "Yes?"

"From here we can't tell what they are," Todd said. "Just two lights that look about the same."

He sighed deeply. "I guess the only way to tell which one you want to end up at is to get close enough to see clearly what each of them is. Then you can make a wise decision between the two. It's hard to decide this far away."

Like a secret decoder wheel, Christy's thoughts spun furiously, trying to figure out Todd's message.

This has to do with Rick. Todd must think he and Rick are like the two lights. What did he say? I have to get close enough to make a wise decision.

Christy moved a little closer to Todd, and he responded by holding her hand a little tighter. Her thoughts came tumbling together, and she quickly lined them up to give Todd a clear response.

She'd tell him she agreed and thought this time in Maui would be perfect for them to get to know each other better than ever and to get closer and closer to each other. If he would make some kind of gesture or some kind of statement to Paula, then she would know he wasn't interested in her games, and he only wanted to spend time with Christy. Then all their difficulties would be cleared up.

Before she could tell him all that, he let go of her hand, sprang from his seat, and with a look of little-boy excitement, he said, "That's what I'll do! I'll just keep going, and I'll ask God to show me which one to choose. It'll get clearer, the closer I get!"

He looked so pleased, but Christy felt so confused. She thought the hidden message of the island-lights was directed at her, when Todd really must have been thinking about a decision he was trying to make. But what decision?

"I'm turning in for the night," Bob called out to them, switching off the TV.

"I'm right behind you," Todd said.

He took one more glance over his shoulder at the lights and then offered a hand to Christy. She took it and wanted to pull him back to the chair so they could keep talking and living out her birthday wish. But Todd pulled her up to a standing position, and she could see more clearly in the soft light how pleased he was with his "lights on the island" analogy.

"Man, I'm glad we saw those two lights. It really clears things up for me. Hey, don't forget your presents." Todd picked up the straw beach bag Mom had given her so she could fill it with the other gifts. "I'll see you in the morning."

After Christy gathered her things, Todd disappeared into the room he shared with David. She walked back to the next-door condo with a sunken heart.

Why was our magical time cut off so suddenly? It was like my birthday wish only came half true.

Paula and Mom were already asleep, so she quietly got ready for bed. While brushing her teeth, she remembered the conversation she had had with herself in the mirror that morning.

What's my problem? This has been an incredible birthday! The best I've ever had. How come I'm never happy with what I get? I got my wish, to be with Todd. I got a promise of a car and a surprise call from Rick. I just spent my sixteenth birthday in Hawaii; so why am I feeling so discontented?

She lay awake a long time that night, sorting out everything. What was Todd deciding? Were the two lights her and another girl? It couldn't be Paula, could it? And why did he ask her about Rick? Would Todd object if she told him she was going out with Rick in August?

As far as Christy could see, all along she and Todd were free to go out with other people. Todd had taken another girl named Jasmine out to dinner the night of his senior prom. Christy hadn't ever really gone on a formal date with Todd, like out to dinner, since her parents didn't allow her to date. Now that she was sixteen, finally she could date.

But what if Todd wanted to go steady? Then she couldn't go out with Rick, or could she?

Todd would never ask her to go steady.

What if Rick wanted to go steady? Then she couldn't go out with Todd anymore.

The more she thought, the more complicated it all became. She decided her life was actually easier when she was younger, because she didn't have to make all these decisions. She never did like making decisions!

In the darkness of her room, Christy felt her forever bracelet and remembered her warm feeling when Todd held her hand and stroked the bracelet. That opened another string of questions.

Did that bracelet already mean they were going steady?

Christy turned on her side and pulled the sheet up to her chin. What if her mom was right, and some other guy was out there for her that she hadn't even met yet?

An idea came to Christy, and she responded to it

immediately. She jumped out of bed and tiptoed into the bathroom with her purse. Closing the door softly, she turned on the light. She scrounged through her purse, looking for a piece of paper.

The first thing she found was the mysterious letter she'd never asked Paula about. Could it have been from Rick? No, he would have said something when he called her tonight. Besides, it looked like a girl's handwriting. Christy left it on the bathroom counter so she would remember to ask Paula in the morning.

Then she pulled out her notepad, the one with a picture of Garfield surfing on the front. Christy had intended to write out her feelings, the way she often did in her diary. But now, sitting on the floor with her back against the bathroom wall, listening to the never-ending surf outside the bathroom window, she had a different idea.

She hesitated, chewing on the eraser and curling and uncurling her toes. Then she released her insecurities and let what she felt deep in her heart appear on paper.

Dear Future Husband,

I turned sixteen today, and I know it may seem weird writing this to you now, but this letter is sort of my way of making a promise to you in writing.

Maybe I already know you, or maybe we haven't met yet. Either way, I want to save myself for you. I want my whole self, my heart and body and everything, to be a present I'll give you on our wedding day.

I don't care how long it takes or how hard it gets, but I promise you I won't let anybody else "unwrap" me, so on our wedding night I'll be the kind of gift you'll be happy to receive.

I know I have a lot of years ahead of me before we get married, whoever you are. That's why I want to make this promise now, so that no matter whom I go out with, I'll always think of myself as a present I want to give to you alone one day.

I also want to start to pray for you, wherever you are, whoever you are, that God will be preparing you for me and that you'll save all of yourself for me too.

I already love you.

Your future wife,

Christina Juliet Miller

Chapter 9

Mosquito Nets and Prayers

I tried to tell you!" Christy snapped back as Paula complained about her sunburn the next day. "You should've used sunscreen like everyone told you. Have you seen your lips? They look like they bubbled up overnight."

"So, Little Miss Perfect?" Paula sat on her bed's edge, holding a damp washcloth on her chest and letting her words fly fast and furious. "You can't tell me you've never been sunburned in your life! You know what your problem is, Christy? You think you're so right about everything.

"You weren't like this before you got your Christianity, or whatever you call it. You used to be fun to be around. Now you're just a spoiled little brat who goes around condemning everyone because that person isn't perfect, like you."

"I do not!"

"Yes, you do! You and your perfect little dream world. I'm so sure! Who else writes letters to their future husbands?" Her voice turned into a whine, "I'm saving my body for you, honey. It's a perfect gift for you alone!"

Christy sprang from her bed and rescued her Garfield notepad, which she had left on the bathroom counter and

Paula had obviously found this morning.

Wagging the notepad in front of Paula, she warned, "That was really rude, Paula! Stop being such a big snoop and leave my stuff alone."

"Hey, hey!" Mom broke up the confrontation. "What's going on here?"

Neither of them spoke. Their eyes flashed the remainder of their angry messages back and forth where Mom couldn't see.

Mom looked first at Christy, then at Paula and with a calm, motherly voice said, "I suppose this was bound to happen. You two always were more like sisters than friends. Why don't you each try giving the other some space this morning, okay?"

"Fine with me," Paula said firmly.

Mom took a good look at Paula and said, "You must stay out of the sun today, Paula. You overdid it yesterday, and you'll make yourself sick. Now you two settle your differences and give each other some space."

Mom folded her arms and waited for them to respond.

"Sorry," Christy offered meekly.

"Sorry," Paula mumbled the expected word like a young schoolgirl.

Satisfied, Mom walked away. Christy held up the notepad to Paula and whispered between her teeth, "Stay out of my stuff."

"Don't leave your 'stuff' lying around."

Christy grabbed her clothes and marched off to the bathroom to change. As soon as she soundly shut the door, the accusations came at her for being such a horrible

Christian and a poor example of a best friend. She was supposed to be witnessing to Paula, not alienating her!

The guilt feelings hung on her all day. She went swimming in the pool and then in the ocean with David until about noon. Then, without interrupting Paula, who had set up her own little camp on the couch, where she spent the day watching TV, Christy showered and changed and joined Mom and Marti for lunch in Lahaina.

They meandered through shop after shop along Front Street and ended up at an open-air restaurant, where they ate salads at a table right by the water.

Mom and Marti chatted about all the boats they could see in Lahaina Harbor. Then they started in about some uncle Christy didn't even know who had had his gall bladder removed.

Christy tuned them out and watched the dozens of tiny crabs skittering across the rocks below them. The afternoon was kind of dreamy and the setting like something from a movie.

While shopping, Christy had enjoyed the bright-colored tropical birds they had seen pacing up and down their perches like a pirate's first mate. And she loved the plumeria trees down by the little public library. They filled the hot afternoon air with a heavy, sweet fragrance.

However, it didn't matter how charming the town was or how exotic the afternoon air smelled. She felt miserable.

It seems like a cruel joke, she told the uncaring crabs over the railing, *to be here with Todd and Paula—the two people I consider my best friends—and to feel so lonely. I know, Todd had to paint today, and he didn't go surfing this morning, so I wasn't able to spend any time with him. But I*

*want to find out what he was talking about last night. What
is he trying to decide?*

*As far as Paula goes, I wish she'd never come. I wish
she'd stayed in Wisconsin, and we could let our childhood
memories be the way we think of each other. We've both
changed too much to try to be friends now.*

I wish Katie had come instead of Paula.

"Ready for some more shopping?" Marti asked, breaking
into Christy's grumbling thoughts.

"I guess so."

"Don't you need to get a few more gifts for your
friends?" Marti prompted.

"Yeah, I'd like to find something to take back to Katie."

"It's too bad Paula couldn't have come shopping with
us," Marti said, counting out the dollar bills she planned to
leave as a tip.

"She needed a day to catch her breath," Mom said.
"What with the jet lag, time change and horrible sunburn, I
think she needed a day of complete rest."

"Whatever you find for Katie, why don't you get the
same thing for Paula?" Marti suggested.

Christy didn't want to. She didn't want to do Paula any
favors. After all, Paula hadn't done any for her!

She ended up buying a white-shell bracelet for Paula at
the very first shop they stopped in. Actually, Marti bought
it. She picked it out too. To keep Marti happy, Christy
agreed Katie wasn't a bracelet kind of person, but Paula
would probably be thrilled with it. So Marti bought it, and
Christy hoped that would be the end of that.

A few shops later, Christy found a University of Hawaii T-shirt for Katie. Marti insisted on buying three of them so Paula, Katie and Christy could all match. Christy agreed as long as she could pick out three different colors, which she did, reserving the pink one for herself.

For fun, she also bought a grass hula skirt to take back to Katie.

With hands full of shopping bags, they headed back to where they'd parked the van. They passed an old, two-story, white house with green trim and a sign in front that said, "Baldwin Missionary Home, 1836, Museum Open Daily."

"Could we go in there?" Christy asked.

"It's only an old house turned into a museum," Marti explained. "Missionaries built it when they first came here. I don't think you'd find it very interesting, Christy."

"Yes, I would. It looks like a neat house. I'd like to go on the tour."

"So would I," Mom said.

For some reason, Marti looked annoyed.

"Go ahead. You have to pay for the tour; it's not free." The way she said it, Christy thought it must be a huge fee. "I'll wait here on the bench."

Mom and Christy paid their admission fee of two dollars.

Christy thought, *You are so funny, Aunt Marti. You left more money than this on the table for a tip!*

The inside of the house looked very American, not tropical at all. There were wooden floors, four-poster beds, blue and white china on the large wooden table and handmade patchwork quilts on the beds.

The tour began in the bedroom, where Christy noticed the large mosquito nets hanging over the bed. The tour guide explained that the missionaries were not popular with the sailors, who harbored here every winter, because they discouraged the sailors' immoral life-style.

"It's said no mosquitos were on the islands," the guide stated, "until some sailors tried to get back at the missionaries by dumping a barrel of brackish water into the canal that used to run behind the missionaries' home. The barrel came over on a ship from Mexico and was teaming with mosquito larvae. Hence, mosquitos made their home on the islands."

One of the women in their little tour group snorted and said, "What a foolish thing to do!"

The guide went on, "The missionaries were fired on as well but survived the attack. Mind you, this was not the Hawaiian natives attacking them, but their fellow Americans."

"How did they respond?" someone in the group asked. "Did they retaliate?"

The guide smiled as if she'd been asked that question before. "You must keep in mind, these were God-fearing, New-England Christians. They stood their ground on what they believed to be right, morally and biblically. It's been said their only retaliation was to pray for their enemies."

During the rest of the tour, Christy only took in parts of the guide's sentences. She had become absorbed with the thought that, as God-fearing Christians, the missionaries prayed for their enemies.

Todd said he prayed everyday for Alissa, and he had told Christy she should pray for Paula. Even though she had agreed with Todd and thought it was a good idea, she hadn't prayed for Paula once since then. Not that Paula was truly an enemy. She was a friend, just like the American sailors should have been friends with the American missionaries, but their moral standard separated them. In a way, Christy had felt that separation from Paula over her choice of bathing suits and her goal to lose her virginity.

When they rejoined Marti and strolled back to the car, Christy imagined Lahaina's streets, alive with crusty, drunken sailors hurling insults at a pious, missionary woman in her long-sleeved dress with her bonnet tipped down, praying for them as she passed by.

All Christy could think about was how much she wanted to talk to Todd about all this, to get his perspective on how to pray. It was one thing for him to tell her she should pray for her friend, and another thing to teach her how.

When they arrived at the huge, shady, banyan tree, Marti insisted they cross the street and enter the Lahaina Wharf Cinema Center. She led them to the lower level, marching like a woman who knew right where she was going. Apparently she did, because they entered a shop labeled, "T.C.B.Y."—The Country's Best Yogurt.

Marti briskly announced, "This is the only frozen yogurt I'll eat. Their white chocolate mousse is absolutely divine. Order what you like. I'm paying."

Christy ordered a small chocolate from the friendly, dark-haired guy behind the counter.

"Would you like a topping?" he asked, his white smile peeking out from under his moustache. "The macadamia nuts are really *'ono* on the chocolate yogurt."

" *'Ono?*" Christy asked.

"The best," he said, lifting the ladle, ready to scoop the nuts onto her yogurt.

Christy hated nuts. She had always hated nuts. She used to suck the coating off M&M's peanuts and throw the peanuts away. At this very moment, though, Christy felt adventuresome.

"Sure, go ahead," she said. "I'll try the macadamia nuts."

The guy was right. They were *'ono!* As she scraped the last spoonful out of her cup, she felt proud of herself for trying something new. Todd would be proud of her.

Back at the condo, Christy found Paula napping and Todd still painting, so she joined David on the couch at Bob and Marti's condo and watched the end of some cartoon. Within minutes she dozed off and was awakened almost an hour later by Marti, who suggested they all go for an evening stroll on the beach.

Christy shook herself awake and, with a string of yawns, found her thongs and joined Marti, Mom and David by the front door. Todd, freshly showered and in clean shorts and a windsurfing T-shirt, stepped out of the kitchen as Christy was smoothing down her hair.

He gave Christy a smile and said, "Looks like you had a good nap."

She could have taken his comment as an insult to her appearance but decided not to take offense. "I really conked out."

"Bob is going to stay and clean up," Marti said, "and

Paula said she'd rather not go this time, so we're all set."

Todd walked next to Christy to the elevator. As she began to wake up, all her afternoon thoughts came back to her, and she was anxious to talk them through with Todd. Even though it was a little thing, she couldn't wait to tell him she had eaten nuts on her yogurt.

"I think I'll stay behind," Todd suddenly announced as the elevator door opened, and they all filed in. "I'll check on Paula and help Bob finish up."

With that, the door sealed, and the elevator lowered them to the ground level.

"If Todd's not going, then I don't want to go," David stated. "I'm going back up."

"You don't need to go back, David," Mom said. "Stay with us. Help me find some shells."

"I don't want to go!" David whined. "Can't I go back up, please?"

"Of course you can," Marti answered for Mom.

The elevator stopped at the bottom floor where Mom, Marti and Christy exited and David shot back up to the sixth floor. Christy could feel Mom watching her, trying to read her feelings, but Christy kept them hidden.

It was impossible, though, for her to enjoy the sunset or the way the warm sand slipped between her toes, knowing that Paula and Todd were alone together. It seemed like a very long walk. Mom and Marti contentedly collected tiny shells, and Christy followed along, bending occasionally to snatch a shell and drop it into her shorts' pocket without even looking at it.

When Marti stopped by the condo pool on the way back and began to talk to some people, Christy went on up to the condo. Bob was washing out paintbrushes.

"Hi," she said, hiding her anxiety and distrust. "Where is everybody?"

"I sent Todd across the street for pizza. Paula may have gone with him. David's in the shower." He added with a grin, "But then, you weren't really worried about David, were you?"

Christy smiled and went back to her room to check her appearance in the mirror. A little more makeup, a few more brushes to make her hair fuller, a squirt of perfume. There. If Todd was trying to make a decision between the two of them, she would do her best to make it an easy choice.

"Pizza's here!" Christy heard Mom call, and she stepped out of her room to find everyone gathered on their lanai to eat.

Paula, apparently revived from the day's rest, had turned back into her bubbly, fun-loving self and was sitting on the arm of Todd's chair, gingerly biting into a slice of pizza.

Christy plopped a slice of pizza on a paper plate and took the only spot left, the lounge chair. She felt as if she were separated from the rest of them by an invisible screen. Lively conversation hummed around the table, but no one directly addressed her.

How can I sit here with my family and friends and feel hopelessly lonely?

Todd excused himself as soon as he had downed three large pieces of pizza. "See you all in the morning," he said.

Bob looked at his watch. "Nine o'clock already! No

wonder I'm so tired. Todd, why don't you take tomorrow off? We pretty well finished up the painting today. I can do the rest myself tomorrow."

Todd stood by the sliding screen door. "Cool. Might be a good day to go to Hana. Good night, everyone."

How can you do that, Todd? How can you go a whole day without saying more than one sentence to me?

Todd had spent the whole day around Paula. Was it part of his decision-making process? Maybe he had planned to spend all that time with her to get closer to her so he could decide whom he liked more.

The rest of Christy's pizza went uneaten.

"Where's Hana?" Mom asked.

Bob explained that Hana was a small community on the other side of the island and that Todd had mentioned his dad had taken him camping there years ago.

"Sounds like a fun trip for the kids," Marti suggested. "They can take the Jeep, and Margaret and I can get some more shopping in."

"Settled," Bob stated, eyeing the last piece of pizza. "Anybody want another piece?"

Christy excused herself and went to bed, choosing the agony of loneliness over the chance of another confrontation with Paula. She knew she should read her Bible and pray before she went to sleep, but she didn't want anyone to think she was awake. She lay still for a long time, with her face to the wall. When she did fall asleep, she dreamed about the lonely life of the virtuous missionary woman in Lahaina long ago.

Chapter 10

Which Way to the Waterfalls?

The next morning Paula acted as if no tension had ever existed between the two of them. She complimented Christy on her hair as they shared the bathroom and asked Christy to put some aloe vera gel on her back.

The raging red of Paula's skin two days ago had toned down to a tender pink, and her shoulders had begun to peel.

"I should've listened to you," Paula admitted. "I've never been sunburned like this before."

"Well, I have to admit that when I went to California last summer Marti kept telling me to use sunscreen, and I didn't. I got burned too. I even spent a day on the couch, just like you did. Only I moaned a lot more, and the only thing I did all day was sip ice water."

Paula laughed. "Why didn't you tell me!"

"I don't know. You were so set on getting a tan. Some things I guess people have to figure out for themselves."

"Christy, that's exactly what I've been wanting to tell you." Paula met Christy's gaze in the bathroom mirror. "You should know me well enough to know I'm the kind of person who likes to figure things out for herself. I mean,

136

you might be right about the sunscreen and maybe about some other things. But I have to figure them out for myself. That's just the way I am."

"I know. I'm that way too," Christy said.

"No, you don't understand," Paula said. "What I mean is, do us both a favor and stop bugging me about becoming religious."

"Becoming religious!"

Paula's tone heightened. "You haven't stopped bugging me since last summer. First in all your letters, and now that we're together, you're so righteous about everything. I still can't believe you brought my old bathing suit along! You have such a perfect little standard for living.

"That's fine for you. And you could even be right about God and everything. But I have to figure it out myself."

Christy blinked but didn't respond.

Paula looked down and pulled her mascara from her cosmetic bag, untwisting the top and jamming the wand in and out. "I've wanted to say that ever since I got here, and I'm glad I finally did, especially since we're going to be together all day."

She began to apply her mascara, and Christy could see Paula's hand was shaking.

"So, if it's okay with you, let's go back to being friends the way we've always been and let me figure out my life and make my own mistakes."

Silence hung between them for a moment. Then Christy broke through the stalemate by swishing out of the bathroom and into the bedroom. She began to toss things into the straw beach bag Mom had given her.

I'm just trying to help you, Paula, and you don't even see it. We're so different now! Things that are important to me mean nothing to you. How can I let you live your life when I see you about to make some major mistakes?

With deliberate steps, Christy marched to the linen closet and yanked out a couple of beach towels. Hugging the towels, she closed her eyes, took a deep breath and tried to exhale all her frustrations.

"She's not pau." Todd's words from earlier came back to Christy. *"You should be praying for her."*

Just as she was about to piece together a prayer for Paula, David and Todd bounded through the open door. With ice chest in hand and the Jeep keys between his teeth, Todd jerked his head toward the door, motioning Christy to come.

Paula appeared, bright and smiling, and Christy decided she wouldn't let anything ruin this day. Even when Paula snatched the front seat of the Jeep and settled in, smiling at Todd, Christy made a deliberate effort not to let it get to her.

The four of them sailed down the road with the wind in their hair. It was impossible to hear anyone speak until they came into Lahaina and Todd took a right turn toward the center of town.

"You want to see the first church the missionaries built here?" Todd asked. "I used to walk past it everyday on my way home from school."

"I thought we were going to the waterfalls," David griped.

"Yeah," Paula agreed as Todd drove slowly through a small intersection and into a part of town with lots of old wood houses lining the narrow street.

"I'd like to see it," Christy said firmly.

"There's the church right there," Todd said, stopping the Jeep under some tall palm trees next to a low stone wall. A sign in front said "Waine'e Church."

"This actually isn't the original one. The first one blew down, and they rebuilt it. Then I think it blew down or burned down again. The missionaries never gave up, though. They kept rebuilding the church. This one stayed, because they built it the right way, facing the mountains. That way when the Kona winds came, all they had to do was open the front and back doors and let the wild wind blow right through, out to the ocean. Pretty good thinking, huh?"

Paula gave a yawn.

Todd smiled and started up the engine. He looked at Christy over his shoulder and said, "I studied all this when I was growing up here. I forget not everybody is as interested in the early missionaries as I am."

"I am!" Christy said, eagerly leaning forward. "My mom and I toured the missionary house."

"The Baldwin House on Front Street?"

"Yes, I really like it." Christy felt an air of satisfaction, knowing she had one up on Paula.

"The very first missionary was Reverend Richardson." Todd pointed to the graveyard next to the church as he slowly pulled out onto the road. "He's buried right there. An amazing man. They say he singlehandedly stopped the epidemic of small pox from wiping out Lahaina, and he wasn't even a doctor."

"Wow," Christy said, enjoying Todd's full attention.

"Is this going to turn into a historical tour?" Paula interjected. "Or are we going to the waterfalls?"

"Yeah!" David protested.

"Okay, okay," Todd said as the Jeep connected with the main highway, and they sped on toward the other side of the island.

Christy sat back, satisfied, knowing she and Todd could talk more about the missionaries later, just the two of them, an interest Paula didn't share.

She felt something more than a shared interest with Todd in the missionaries. She couldn't explain why, but she felt awed and thrilled when she thought about men and women who loved God so much they didn't give up, even when their church blew down. She had admired their perseverance when she toured the Baldwin House.

A little way past the airport, they slowed to go down what appeared to be the main street of a funky-looking little town. Just before they reached the town, Todd shouted, "Right up here is the wind-surfing capital of the world. You guys want to stop and watch?"

"No!" David answered. "Not unless we can go swimming there."

Todd smiled over his shoulder. "Okay, David. We'll get you to a waterfall. Hang on. It's going to be a long, winding road."

During the next few miles, the road became narrower and narrower. Around every bend and curve, they met another bend and curve.

Christy thought it all looked like she imagined old Hawaii to have been—waterfalls tucked behind valleys that were carpeted with huge ferns. Bright flowers literally grew out of the rocks; exotic birds sang in the overhanging trees; and every now and then, simple, little, tin-roofed homes built up on stilts appeared.

Being in the open Jeep, everything seemed close up, like she could pick a flower or fern as they passed, if she were quick enough.

The scenery stayed like that for mile after winding mile. On they traveled, bump after bump, curve after curve, sliding through tight spots in the road. Twice they had to stop and back up so an oncoming car could get by. Christy figured they must have driven for more than three hours already.

"Can't they do something about improving this road?" Paula exclaimed after a swift curve brought her dangerously close to the jagged, volcanic rock wall on her side of the Jeep.

"Actually, they have," Todd said. "When my dad and I used to come out here camping, it was much worse."

"Worse!" Paula squeaked. "How could it be worse?"

"Parts of it weren't paved. It was gravel and dirt and lots of mud when it rained."

"They sure don't make it very appealing for a tourist to come all the way out here," Paula said.

Todd smiled and nodded. "I think that's the idea. The locals like it unchanged. I don't blame them. Hana is a unique place."

"Are we almost there yet?" David asked for what seemed like the fiftieth time.

"Almost."

About fifteen minutes later, the Jeep hit smooth pavement and wider road. They knew they were in Hana by the community of small houses that suddenly appeared on the hillside.

Christy spotted an old white church with a tall steeple and smiled to see that the undaunted missionaries had found their way to remote Hana more than a century ago. Across the road from the church lay a huge, fenced pasture with a carpet of emerald grass running all the way to steep cliffs. The cliffs dropped into the bright turquoise ocean. The blending of colors struck her as incredibly beautiful.

A dozen or so horses nibbled on the rich green grass, their shiny coats looking more silky in the tropical sun than any horse she had ever seen.

She felt twinges of homesickness for the farm she grew up on in Wisconsin. But Wisconsin grass never turned this dazzling shade of green, and horses back on the farm were merely black or brown. Not silky ebony, amber and caramel like these.

"Where are the waterfalls?" David whined.

Instead of answering, Todd swung the Jeep into a tiny, old-fashioned gas station and filled the tank.

David whined the whole time. "I'm hungry. When are we going to eat? How much farther is it? Can't we get out here?"

"David, stop it! You sound like a big baby," Paula scolded. "We shouldn't have let you come with us."

Before Todd got back in, he roughed up David's already wind-snarled hair and said, "Think you can hang in there another half hour, dude?"

"A half hour!" David squawked.

"I'm so sure! I thought we were almost there," Paula moaned. "You didn't tell us it would take all day to get there! I thought you said it was like seventy miles."

"It is," Todd explained. "Something like that. But you may have noticed we haven't been driving very fast."

"Then let's get going," Paula ordered. "I can't believe it's the middle of the afternoon, and we're not even there yet. We're barely going to have any time left before we have to turn around and go back."

"Oh, no," David groaned. "Do we have to take the same road back?"

"Unless you want to go the long way back on the dirt road," Todd said, hopping into the front seat and bringing the engine to a roar. "Come on, you guys, where's your sense of adventure?"

"Yahoo!" Christy shouted spontaneously as Todd made the tires peel out on the road.

Christy loved this. She really, truly did. If this was what he meant the other day about being adventurous, then maybe she really was after all.

"Oh, one thing I should tell you," Todd called over his shoulder as they drove under a huge plumeria tree, which filled the air with its rich fragrance. "The road up to the falls is ten times worse than the road we just came over."

Chapter 11

The Bridge

This road should be condemned!" Paula shrieked. "How much farther is it?"

"Not much. Relax, Paula. This is the real Hawaii," Todd said.

"I'd rather be back at the condo," Paula muttered, crossing her arms.

"I like it," Christy called out. They were driving slowly, and the wind had subsided so her voice clearly traveled.

She laughed at her own exuberance and then let loose all her pent up feelings. "Look at this, you guys! It's beautiful. I don't care how long it takes to get there. Look! Have you ever seen flowers growing out of a rock before?" With a daring thrust, she snatched a tiny purple flower.

She sniffed the fragrance and told them all, "I could live here the rest of my life."

Todd glanced at Christy over his shoulder, and she could see his dimple when he smiled. "I knew you'd like it here."

He slowed the Jeep to creep over another one of the many bridges they had crossed. But this bridge was longer, and people were standing on its side, looking over the edge.

"This is it, guys!" Todd announced. "The parking lot is down the road, and then we walk to the falls."

"Finally," David snorted. Then, with a quick look around, he said, "That's all there is? No water slides or anything?"

"Sorry, dude. It's all natural; the way God made it."

From her side of the Jeep, all Christy could see was black rock lining a round pool that flowed into the ocean.

All of a sudden Paula shrieked, and Todd slammed on the brakes.

"He's going to jump!" Paula screamed. "Somebody stop him!"

Too late. A man in fluorescent green trunks sprang from the edge of the old stone bridge and jumped into the water below.

"Oh. There's water down there!" Paula said in a flash of discovery. "I didn't know he was diving into the water!"

"Whoa!" David exclaimed. "Did you see that, Todd? Have you ever done that? Have you ever jumped off that bridge?"

"Not yet."

After they parked, they hiked the long, grassy trail down to the lower pools. Then they waded through the chilly water over the slippery rocks until they came to a gravel spot by a large pool and put down their belongings. Paula laid out her towel and began to sunbathe. David yanked off his T-shirt and glasses in one motion and jumped into the pool.

"Anybody want to go exploring?" Todd asked.

"Not me," Paula said without looking up. "I got enough

Indiana-Jones trailblazing on the ride here."

"I do!" Christy said eagerly and followed Todd over the rocks and into the refreshing water.

Todd motioned to a big black rock and excitedly said, "Here. This is the one. Sit right here. What do you see?"

"It's beautiful," Christy said. "So tropical. I love it!"

What she didn't tell him was she also loved having him all to herself.

"Take your time," he said, placing his foot on the rock next to where she sat. His soggy tennis shoe dripped water on her leg. "Take it all in and tell me if you see it."

Slowly she scanned the tall, black sides of the canyon, covered with foliage hanging down in long vines. She counted three large pools that each flowed into a waterfall into the next pool. A fourth pool stumbled over precarious chunks of black lava before giving itself over completely to the hungry ocean that sent wave after wave to lap up the fresh mountain spring water.

"You mean the colors?" she asked Todd. "The blues are so blue, and the plants are an indescribable shade of green I've never seen before."

"No, no, up there," Todd pointed.

Christy studied the huge volcanic mountain, dressed in a ruffled green gown of wild foliage that flowed down to the canyon where they sat. Then she saw it. It took a minute to place where she had seen that exact scene before. Finally she remembered.

"The bridge! It's the bridge on the poster you gave me. This must be the exact spot they took the picture from."

Todd smiled and nodded, looking pleased that she figured it out. "I found that poster the first day Bob and I were here. In the grocery store, of all places! I bought three. One for me, one for you, and one for my dad."

He wedged himself onto the rock next to Christy and said, "My dad and I sat right here on this same rock when I was about ten years old."

"Really? How neat. That's why you remembered the bridge and bought the posters?"

"There's more to it. Remember the guy who jumped off the bridge when we were going across it?"

"It's the same bridge, right? The one we drove over."

Todd nodded. "My dad jumped off the bridge a couple of times, and he wanted me to jump too. But I never could get up the nerve."

"Well, I don't blame you." Christy tried to sound encouraging. "It's a long way down! How far is it?"

"I don't know. Maybe sixty feet or more. And you have to land in a certain spot where it's deep enough, because lots of rocks are hidden underwater. Kimo came with us one time. He jumped. But I couldn't do it. I thought my dad would be disappointed in me, you know, that I wasn't a real man or something because I wouldn't jump."

"You were only ten years old."

"Kimo was ten too." Todd looked at Christy.

She turned away from the bridge and met his gaze. His eyes looked as blue as the sky. As blue as the ocean. As blue as the fresh-water pool at her feet. It hit her in that moment, looking into his eyes, that there was so much she didn't know about Todd and so much she wanted to know.

"So, what happened?" Christy asked, feeling a tiny bit nervous, with Todd sitting so close and looking at her so intently. Yet at the same time she wished they could sit there all afternoon and talk and talk and talk.

"My dad brought me over to this rock, and we sat here just like this. He told me to look at the bridge and always remember it, because my life would be full of bridges. With every bridge would come a choice. Then he told me he admired me because I didn't jump just because Kimo did."

"Wait a minute," Christy interrupted. "He said he admired you for not jumping?"

"Yeah. He said, 'I don't care if you ever jump off that bridge. All that matters to me is that you make your own decision and follow through on it because it's your choice, not because anyone influenced or persuaded you to do it,' or something like that."

Todd paused, and Christy could see this moment meant as much to him as it did to her.

"Anyway, I've never forgotten that day and what my dad said. I think I became more of an individualist after that, making my choices because that's what I chose to do, not because someone cornered me into it."

Todd stood up, reached for Christy's hand, pulled her to her feet and said, "Come on, I'll show you the trail up to the top."

Christy slipped on the first rock, then regained her balance and kept holding tightly to Todd's hand as he led the way up a narrow trail on the rocks. They wound their way under the jungle-growth of huge leaves and trailing vines

.

The pools on their right side grew smaller and more distant the farther up they climbed.

Halfway up, in a clearing, Todd stopped and called down to Paula. She lifted her head from her beach towel and looked all around. Not being able to determine where Todd's voice was coming from, she laid back down and closed her eyes to soak up some more sun.

Christy thought Paula probably couldn't see them without her glasses anyway. Knowing Paula, she probably left them back at the condo with the unused one-piece bathing suit.

David, who had joined some local boys in the shallow water, was busy watching his new friends catch prawns with their homemade metal cages.

Todd and Christy kept climbing until the trail met the road, and Christy realized they were at the top. At the bridge. A few cars passed slowly, and two older ladies stood at the side, cautiously holding onto the railing while snapping pictures of the pools and the ocean.

Todd led Christy along the bridge's edge, looking into the water far below. He stopped at what seemed to be his chosen spot, a few feet from the old ladies. He let go of Christy's hand.

She caught something in his expression and carefully said, "Todd?"

His silver-blue eyes locked onto hers, and she knew he was going to do it. Todd was going to jump.

"You don't have to, you know," she fumbled. "Like your dad said, it has to be your decision, not a whim or a pressure thing."

Todd firmly grasped Christy by the shoulders and pulled her close as a car passed inches behind them. His eyes were swimming with the secret dreams of his heart, and she knew he spoke the truth before he even said the words.

"This is my decision. I'm not doing it for my dad or Kimo or anybody. This is for me."

He broke into a wide grin and said, "In case I don't come up, the keys to the Jeep are in my backpack."

Then he enveloped Christy in his arms and kissed her quickly and firm, like a soldier giving his beloved one last kiss before going off to war.

Before she could respond, Todd released her and positioned himself on the stone railing of the bridge. He set his sights on the small area of deep water below. Without looking back, he bent his knees, and without a sound, Todd launched his six-foot frame into the thick, tropical air.

Chapter 12

Hana After It Rains

Ahhhhhhhh!" screamed one of the old women on the bridge's edge.

Her friend frantically waved her arms and shouted, "Someone save him! He jumped! A man jumped off the bridge!"

Christy, clawing her fingers into the stone railing as she leaned over as far as she dared, held her breath and waited for the splash.

Splash!

Then she counted and frantically scanned the water's surface, watching for Todd's sandy blonde hair to pop up. *Three . . . four . . . five . . . six . . . Come on, Todd! How long are you going to stay down there? Seven . . . eight . . . There he is! There he is! He's okay! He did it!*

Christy reached over and touched the arm of the old woman, who was still screaming and waving her hands to the passing cars. Her friend had trotted down the road, hollering and trying to flag down a car.

"Look!" Christy pointed, trying to get the woman's attention. "He's okay! See him down there?"

Todd, treading water in the center of the pool, called out to Christy with hoots and hollers, waving wildly.

Christy stretched her arms over the edge so Todd could see her applauding him.

"Thelma," the woman on the bridge called, "he's all right! Come see!"

Thelma bustled back to the edge and peered over. Todd waved at her with both arms.

"Oh, my heavens!" Thelma sighed. "That young man gave me quite a scare!"

Then turning to Christy she said, "Whatever possessed him to do that?"

"He wanted to," Christy defended. "He knew what he was doing. He's been here before . . . with his dad."

The women did not look impressed, nor did they join Christy in applauding him. Rather, they clutched their cameras, linked arms and cautiously made their way off the bridge.

Christy heard one of them mutter, "These young people today . . ."

"Hey, Christy!" Todd yelled. "You coming in? The water feels great!"

"I think I'll take the trail down," she called to him. "I'll meet you down there."

"Sure you don't want to jump?"

Christy shook her head briskly, waved once more, then quickly made her way off the bridge and down the narrow trail. It was much harder going down alone, without Todd holding her hand. She lost her footing and landed on her rear end. No one was around to see her, so her embarrassment quickly disappeared, and she proceeded with greater caution.

Arriving at the trail's end, she stepped into the shallow water and gingerly placed her feet on the slippery rocks. She stopped to rest on the rock she and Todd had sat on earlier.

David stood only a few feet away, fishing with something tied to the end of a string.

"Hey, Christy! Where have you been? Some guy jumped off the bridge. Did you see him?" David asked.

"Yep, I saw him, all right. You know who it was?"

"Who?"

"Todd."

"No way!"

"Yes way, David. Ask him yourself."

"Where is he?"

"Hey!" Todd called out from the gravel spot where they had left their small ice chest and towels. "Anybody else want some lunch?"

Paula sat right next to Todd on a towel. It seemed to Christy Paula scooted closer when Christy approached.

"Hey, Todd!" David called out. "Did you really jump?"

Todd took a deep breath and let out a poof of air before saying, "Yeah, dude. I really jumped."

Christy thought he looked and sounded as if he still didn't believe it himself.

"There's probably not much left," Paula said, poking her hand in the ice chest. "Your little brother got into it and started taking the meat out of the sandwiches to use for bait."

"I only opened one sandwich," David defended.

As usual, Uncle Bob had supplied a generous portion of everything, and they had plenty to eat. They all talked about Todd's jump while they ate.

Christy became so hot sitting in the sun that, when she finished her sandwich, she stepped down the natural rock-steps into the deep pool to cool off. At first, the water felt freezing cold against her sun-baked legs. It felt miserable to be half cold and half hot, so taking a deep breath, she stretched her arms in front of her and took the plunge.

"Brrrr!" she called to the others when she surfaced. "Verrrrrry refrrrrrrreshing!"

"You convinced me." Todd sprang to his feet and did a shallow dive off the side, coming up right next to Christy.

"You're right!" he said, blinking as he surfaced. "It's refreshing. Come on, Paula! It'll wake you up."

"No, thanks."

"Come on," Todd nudged. "You can't drive all this way to Kipahulu and not even go in the water!"

"I went in already."

"What? Up to your ankles?" Christy teased.

"If you won't come in the water, we'll have to bring the water to you!" Todd hoisted himself out of the pool and grasped Paula by the wrists.

She began to kick and scream, trying to pull away so Todd wouldn't throw her in. He, of course, overpowered her, and with a typically loud Paula-screech, she landed in the pool with Todd going in with her.

They came up laughing and splashing water at each other. Christy fought hard to resist the urge to crawl out of the water and curl up on a rock by herself.

"Hey," Todd called out, circling Christy in with his remark, "you ever been underneath a waterfall before?"

"I want to go!" David yelled from the shore and then jumped in to join them.

Todd motioned with his head toward the waterfall, and Christy swam after him along with the other two, telling herself this was too wonderful a place to sit alone feeling sorry for herself. The roaring noise and the carefree spray on her face made her feel excited and nervous the closer they came to the waterfall.

"It's easier to go in this way," Todd directed. "Follow me."

They all swam around to the side and pressed their backs against the rock until they could slide into a hollowed out part of the rock. Slowly inching along, they found a ledge to sit on directly behind the waterfall with the rock-overhang sheltering them like a thick, black umbrella.

"This is incredible!" Christy said, her words echoing in the cavern. "Look how the water comes down like a thick sheet of glass and then shatters into a billion, foaming bubbles when it hits the water."

"There's a much bigger waterfall about a mile and a half up the trail, and you can go behind that one too," Todd said, his deep voice resounding in the hollow.

"Let's go there," Christy suggested.

"He said it was more than a mile, Christy. You want to walk that far? I think we'd better start to drive back. What time is it?" Paula was shivering and not enjoying the novelty of sitting behind a waterfall at all.

"We probably should get going," Todd agreed. "If we stay too long we'll have to drive that road in the dark."

"No, thank you!" Paula spouted. "I'm going back to dry off."

"Can't we stay a little longer?" David moaned. "I haven't caught anything yet."

They followed Todd out the side of the waterfall, and Christy was amazed at how much easier it was to hear, the farther they swam from the crashing falls. Swimming back, Todd agreed to help David try to catch his illusive pet prawn.

The girls dried off, and Paula fished for her camera in Christy's bag and began to snap off the roll of pictures. Christy watched David and Todd hunt for the prawns, which looked like miniature lobsters, about three to seven inches long.

The prawns hid themselves well under the rocks, but the lunch meat tied to the string on David's stick beckoned them to come out of hiding and try to snatch the meat. Todd and David caught two but lost them before they could lift the string out of the water and grab them.

David decided to stand very still in the water next to the rock and grab the critter before it had time to scamper under the rock. It worked. David caught a big one.

Gleefully splashing his way over to Christy and Paula, David proudly showed off the prize in his fist.

"Get that pinchy thing away from me," Paula wailed. "It's gross!"

"He's my new pet," David announced. "Sydney the Shrimp."

"David, you can't keep that thing," Paula said.

"Sure I can. I'm going to keep it in the ice chest with some little rocks and water." David set about to turn the empty ice chest into a new home for Sydney.

Paula looked thoroughly annoyed. "Todd, don't you think we'd better get going? When we first got here lots of other people were around, but now there's hardly anyone."

"Good. Not as much traffic." Todd reached for his towel and backpack and said, "You guys ready?"

Christy scrambled to get her things together and reluctantly slipped her feet back into her cold, soggy tennis shoes.

The four of them waded through the water and over the slippery rocks. The late afternoon shadows darkened the water, making it difficult to find sure footing. David received the assignment of carrying the small plastic ice chest since he had turned it into a prawn playground.

The hike to the parking lot was uphill, and when Christy reached the Jeep, she felt pooped and not at all looking forward to the long ride home. She plopped her beach bag in the front seat, as if to say "Front seat reserved for Christy."

"What are they doing?" Christy asked David as he opened the ice chest to check on his treasure inside.

"Todd said it was some kind of fruit or something, and Paula wanted him to get it. Here. He told me to put his backpack in the car."

Christy shielded her eyes from the sun and watched Todd

climb a tree at the far end of the grassy parking lot. It was too far away, and she was too tired to try to join Paula, who stood below the tree, pointing to the clumps of fruit.

When did they take off, and how come I didn't notice?

Christy decided their delay was to her advantage, and she settled herself in the front seat. She watched them in the rearview mirror.

Todd scaled down the tree and handed Paula the fruit, but suddenly Todd hopped on one foot. Then he grabbed his foot, and from all Christy could see, he fell down or lay down. Paula tossed the fruit into the air and dropped to her knees by his side.

"David, what's going on down there?"

"Where?" David looked around as Christy undid her seat belt.

"I think Todd fell or something." She got out of her seat, and when she saw Paula frantically running toward her, she broke into a run.

"What happened?"

"Backpack!" Paula shrieked. "Where's his backpack?"

She ran past Christy to the Jeep.

"David had it!" Christy started running toward the Jeep with Paula and then on impulse, turned and ran toward the tree where Todd was still lying with his eyes closed.

"What happened? Are you all right?" She fell to her knees and grasped his arm.

Todd opened his eyes and hoarsely said, "Backpack."

"Paula's getting it." Christy glanced over her shoulder. "They're coming. Here they are."

She took his hand in hers and squeezed it.

Paula nearly flung the backpack at Christy's face. "Get it, Christy. He said it's in there. I can't do it!"

"What?" Christy yelped frantically. "What happened? What's in here?"

She tore the zipper open and dumped out the contents.

"A bee!" Paula shrieked. "He got stung, and he's allergic, and he said he'll go unconscious unless he gets a shot!"

Christy grabbed a long, yellow, plastic container that tumbled out of the backpack.

"It must be this thing," she said, taking control of the situation. "Todd? Can you do this? Are you okay?"

"Look at his foot!" David shouted.

Todd's right foot had already swollen twice its normal size.

"Oh, you guys! What are we going to do?" Paula broke into loud sobs. "Is he unconscious?"

"Chris," Todd said in a breathy voice, "do you have the injection?"

Christy popped open the plastic case and removed the hypodermic needle and syringe. "It's right here. What do I do with it, Todd?"

"Take off the cap and hand it to me."

"Oh, I can't look! I can't look! Needles always make me faint!" Paula turned away, still crying.

"Okay, Todd. Here it is. Can you see this okay? I'm putting it in your hand." Christy sounded much braver than she felt.

Todd opened his eyes and pulled himself up. Christy quickly moved behind him to prop him up. He felt like he weighed a thousand pounds. She pressed her shoulder hard against his back to keep him sitting up and closed her eyes while he gave himself the injection.

I feel like I'm going to pass out. Don't do it, Christy. Take a deep breath . . .

Todd's back pressed heavily against her shoulder, and she slowly pulled away so he could lie down.

"Is he going to be okay?" David asked in a small, scared voice.

Todd licked his lips. Beads of perspiration dripped off his forehead. He drew in a deep breath and said in a low voice, "Give me another five minutes."

He took a breath. "Then I'll be fine."

Paula stopped crying and turned to face the others, sniffing and drying her eyes. "He took off his shoes to climb the tree, and when he was coming down, this huge bee—it had to be as big as a moth—buzzed past my head. Then the next thing I knew he must've stepped on it or something, 'cuz he dropped like he'd been shot or something and told me to get his backpack."

"Sorry I scared you," Todd said, opening his eyes halfway. "I'm allergic to bee stings."

"Oh, no, duh!" David said relieving the tension with his comical voice and face. "We all thought you were taking a nap!"

Todd's lips pressed together. "If I keep completely still, I stay conscious longer. It takes a little while for the injection to work. I'll be fine."

"Do you think you can walk?" Christy asked.

"Sure. I'll be fine."

"Christy!" Paula sounded panicked again. "A better question would be, can he drive?"

"Sure. I'll be fine." Todd raised himself up on his elbows, blinked his eyes a few times and shook his head. "If you guys carry my stuff, I think I can make it to the car."

They took it slow. Todd tried to hop on his left foot. A painful grimace distorted his face.

"I've got an idea," Christy said. "Paula, go around on his other side. Here, Todd. Put your arms around us. We'll be your crutches."

They made it to the Jeep, and Todd wedged his tender foot into place on the gas pedal. David raced to conquer the front seat, leaving Christy and Paula sentenced to share the backseat.

At this point, Christy didn't care where she sat. She could tell by Todd's expression that even though he said he would be fine, he really wasn't. He tried hard to sound normal.

"Everybody in? Let's hit it!" He aggressively pressed his bare foot on the gas, and the Jeep sailed over the bumps in the parking lot and onto the narrow road. Right before the bridge, Todd swung into a small turnout. He looped his arms over the top of the steering wheel as if holding onto it for support and sucked in a deep breath.

"It hurts too much, huh?" Paula asked anxiously, pressing in between the two front seats. "You can't drive, can you? What are we going to do? You guys, I think he's going to pass out!"

"I'm not going to pass out. I need to elevate my foot for a few more minutes. Maybe we should hang out here another half hour or so."

"But it's getting dark!" Paula said frantically. "We have to get over the really rough road while it's still light, isn't that what you said?"

Todd stretched out his still red and swollen foot, propping it on the slim dashboard. "We've still got another few hours before the sun sets."

"Then why is it getting so dark?" Paula moaned.

"What's that?" David asked, looking up. "Hey, I think it's starting to rain!"

"Eeeeee!" Christy and Paula both wailed as a sudden attack of rain pellets hammered them.

"Didn't this Jeep come with a cover?" Christy asked, rummaging through her bag for her hooded windbreaker.

"Use your beach towels," Todd instructed, grabbing one off the floor board and draping it over David. "It'll probably only last a few minutes."

"Ahhhhh!" Paula cried. "I'm getting drenched!"

Christy pulled her hood over her head and hunched over so that the torrent of rain hit the middle of her back and flowed into puddles on the seat. She thought it was kind of adventuresome, like a movie she saw once about a woman from New York who got lost in a Colombian jungle and had to hike through the rain and mud with her hero.

Then, as instantly as it began, the warm rain turned off, and the not-so-happy adventurers peered out of their beach-towel tents.

"Look at me! I'm soaked!" Paula fussed. "Everything is soaked!"

Todd was especially wet, since he had given his towel to David and braved the gush with only his T-shirt. He roughed up his short hair, sending out a sprinkle of raindrops. Pixie-like rays of returning sunlight danced through the jungle-growth overhead and teased their way into the Jeep, kissing Christy's damp, bare legs with their warmth.

"It smells like, um, like a . . ." Christy tried to find the right word, as she slipped off her wet windbreaker and shook it over the edge of the Jeep.

"Like Hana after it rains," Todd finished for her, taking in a deep breath. "Once you smell a tropical forest after the rain, you never forget it."

"It smells like mildew, you guys!" Paula was now standing up, toweling down her legs, which turned out to be pointless because the towel was wetter than her legs. "We'd better get out of here before another bucket falls on us! Can you drive yet, Todd?"

One look at his foot gave them all the obvious answer. The swelling was not going down, and the redness seemed to be spreading. Todd didn't answer. They all remained silent, waiting for his conclusion.

Christy broke the silence. "I'll drive."

Todd turned and met her clear eyes and sincere smile.

"She can't drive!" David protested. "She doesn't know how! You'll get us all killed! Can't you drive, Paula?"

"I don't know how to drive a stick shift!" Paula spouted.

"Besides, I can't see more than three feet in front of me without my glasses, and I didn't bring them."

"Christy," David warned, "you can't do it."

Todd kept looking at her and said, "You don't have to, you know."

Christy leaned forward, as if she were talking only to Todd, and said, "I want to. This is my decision. I'm not doing it for you or my dad or anybody else. I'm doing this for me."

A knowing smile lit up Todd's face. "This is your bridge, huh?"

"Yep," Christy answered bravely. "And I'm ready to jump."

"What are you guys talking about?" Paula asked.

Without answering, Christy scooted around the side of the Jeep and opened the door for Todd.

"Mind if I sit there, dude?" Todd said to David, as he hopped around and sent David to the backseat, still protesting that Christy would crash the Jeep if Todd let her drive.

Paula started in, too, about how they should try to call for help at a phone somewhere, wherever they might possibly find a phone in this remote spot, and maybe if they called 911 someone would send a helicopter to rescue them.

Todd positioned his foot on the dashboard and began to explain the gears to Christy.

"Hey," he suddenly said, turning to face the two complainers in the backseat, "could you guys cool it!"

They instantly hushed, and Christy listened carefully to

Todd's instructions, remembering fairly clearly when they practiced driving a stick shift in driver's training.

The engine started on her first try, and Todd pressed down on the gear shift and popped it into reverse for her. "Let up slowly on the clutch and don't worry about trying to go fast."

Flashing back on her day in the church parking lot with her dad, she giggled and said, "Don't worry. Slow is what I do best."

Swallowing her giggles and all her nervousness so they landed in her stomach like a big fizzie, she looked over her shoulder. She cautiously let up on the clutch while pressing slightly on the gas to back up onto the road. The Jeep slipped through the muddy gravel as it powered backward, and Christy slammed on the brakes.

Paula screamed, and David started to plead that they call 911.

Todd ignored them, and placing his hand on top of Christy's as she held the gear shift, he calmly said, "Good. Now this is first gear, right here. Go ahead and give it some gas."

She did, and the Jeep lurched forward, spinning mud and spraying all of them with reddish black mud-freckles.

"You've got it, Chris!" Todd praised over the sound of Paula's squawks. "Go for it! Now put it into second gear, right here."

He moved her hand down and her forever bracelet lightly tapped against the metal gear shift.

They rumbled over the bridge, and Todd squeezed her hand, rubbing the chain on the bracelet with his thumb. He didn't have to say a word. She knew he must be thinking the same thing she was thinking. This was their bridge.

Today they both had changed on this bridge. Todd, for jumping off it, and Christy, for driving over it. It would always be a forever moment for them.

Todd let go, and she placed both hands on the steering wheel in the ten and two position.

"Should I keep it in second gear?" Christy asked while they bounced over the muddy road.

"Yeah, and don't try to go any faster. The curves come up quicker than you think."

Todd was right. The curves kept curving, and the bumps kept bumping. Christy's jaw began to send out shooting pains because she had clenched her teeth so long. With every breath, she drew in the fragrance that the tropical rain had scattered all around them, and even though she was scared, she felt happier than she had ever felt before.

The shadows grew, and Christy squinted to see the road, which never seemed to stay in one place. It rose and fell and turned and, in some places, narrowed so that there was room for only one car. In other places, the passenger side dropped off without a guard rail, hundreds of feet down a slide of angry, paralyzed lava that had been forced to stop there hundreds of years ago by the strong hand of the cool ocean.

For nearly an hour, she used every bit of her courage and skill to conquer the Hana Road. When it was nearly dark, without warning, the tires hit smooth, straight pavement, and they all perked up, knowing they had reached Hana.

"Turn up that way," Todd pointed to a long driveway by a sign that said "Hana Ranch Market." "If they're still open, we can get some supplies for the ride home."

"I'll take anything chocolate," Paula said. "I feel like I desperately need some chocolate about now!"

Todd directed Christy where to turn and where to park, and as soon as she stopped, David and Paula jumped out of the Jeep and ran into the store like released prisoners.

Christy flopped against the back of her seat and let out a gigantic sigh of relief.

"You did it!" Todd praised. He unbent his cramped knee and stretched his greatly improved, bee-stung foot. "You never stop surprising me, Christy." He said it firmly and softly while trying to get his stiff legs out the open door.

Once up on his good leg, he said, "I'm going to call your uncle. I'll meet you inside."

Christy relaxed her tensed legs and repeated the thought, *You never stop surprising me, Christy.* For Todd, that was a compliment. Maybe Todd would never compare her eyes to the Blue Grotto. Maybe he would never take her to a fancy restaurant. But today they had shared an adventure, and Christy knew she would never be the same because of it.

Inside the small store, David said, "I want to get this, Christy!"

He held up a T-shirt with a cartoon drawing of a frantic-looking character driving on a road filled with obstacles. Across the top were the words, "I Survived the Road to Hana."

"Will you get it for me?"

Christy laughed aloud. "Sure, David. I think we all should get one."

They all did and wore them home. The T-shirts were the first thing Marti made a fuss over when they stumbled into the condo at almost midnight—cold, tired, dirty and hungry. All chattering at once, they told the details of their wild adventure.

"And you actually drove, Christy?" Mom looked shocked.

"Only the first hour back. When we stopped in Hana, that's when Todd called you guys, his foot was a lot better. So he drove the rest of the way. We were all wet from the rain, and it got so cold from the wind in that open Jeep!"

"I'll get some hot water going," Marti offered, heading for the kitchen and nearly tripping over the ice chest they had brought in. "We've got hot chocolate here somewhere."

Suddenly Marti shrieked, grabbed the broom and began to pound the floor by the opened ice chest. They all ran into the kitchen just in time to see a lifeless Sydney squished on the floor.

"Aunt Marti," David wailed, "that was my shrimp!"

"Oh, David, don't cry. Your uncle will take you out tomorrow night and buy you a shrimp dinner, won't you, Bob?"

David broke into a bleating-calf cry and ran from the room.

"What did I say?" Marti asked.

They were too busy laughing to answer.

Chapter 13

The God-Thing

The final few days of their vacation breezed by as refreshing and fragrant as the summer trade winds. They lounged by the pool, walked along the beach at sunset, shopped and dined at fancy restaurants. Christy and Paula got along much better than at the trip's beginning.

Their last night in Hawaii, Bob took them all on a sunset-dinner sail on a catamaran. About twenty-five tourists, like themselves, took the cruise.

One of them was a university student from Denmark named Alex. Paula had set her eyes on him the minute he came on board, and within five minutes she had started up a conversation with him.

The two of them talked nonstop the entire trip. It seemed to Christy that Alex was captivated by Paula's Paula-ness.

After they had eaten, Christy left the group and, with rocking steps, made her way to the front of the catamaran. She sat down on the webbed tarp spread across the boat's front.

The sun had just been devoured in three swift bites by the volcano that rose out of the center of the island of Molokai.

All that was left was a halo of red-orange-yellow-pink fuzzy clouds that looked like a huge party napkin, wiping the upturned lips of the greedy, sun-swallowing volcano. The ocean, so blue and clear and inviting, rocked her gently with its never-ending lullaby.

Todd quietly joined her and stretched out on his stomach.

"Hey, look!" he said, pointing to Molokai. "There are the two lights again."

"So, have you decided?" Christy asked, feeling a little coy.

From the way the last few days had gone, Christy figured he had evaluated her and Paula and had made Christy his choice.

"No, I haven't," Todd answered slowly. "I still can't decide if I should go to college in the fall or try to get in on the pro surfing tour."

"*That's* what you're trying to decide?" Christy asked.

Todd looked surprised. "Yeah. What did you think?"

To avoid answering she quickly asked, "You want to be a pro-surfer then?"

"No. I want to be a Bible Translator."

In the twilight, his eyes looked as starry as the darkening sky above them. "My dream is to go to some remote tropical island where the natives have never heard the Gospel. I want to live there, learn their language and translate the Bible into their native tongue."

"You want to be a missionary?" Christy said the word reverently, with the same sense of awe and admiration she felt for the early missionaries to Hawaii.

"Yes." Todd said it like a true island dreamer. "I want to be a missionary."

It all became clear to Christy. She understood Todd better at this moment than ever before. Todd had the same never-stop-trying spirit the missionaries must have had when they kept rebuilding their church. Todd had the same God-fearing heart that prompted the Baldwins to pray for, rather than retaliate against, the sailors who infested their home and their island with mosquitos.

As far as making his home in the jungle, yeah. That fit too. Last summer when they went to Disneyland, Todd's favorite attraction turned out to be the Swiss Family Robinson Tree House. Christy could see that Todd would make an outrageous jungle missionary.

"You know, when we were in Hana," Todd continued, "I started dreaming even more about being a missionary. Swimming in fresh water pools, living off the land, the smell after it rains . . ."

"You'd better make sure you take along a lifetime supply of bee-sting antidote!" Christy warned.

Todd laughed. "Right! Don't leave home without it!"

He suddenly turned serious and said, "You did a great job that day, keeping cool in the emergency and everything. I might not have made it if you weren't there. And I never thanked you for driving the Jeep for me."

"That's okay, Todd. You know I did it as much for me as for you. I now have no fear of taking my driving test. If I can drive the Hana Road, I can drive anywhere!"

Todd laughed along with her and said, "Good missionary training for you, *Kilikina*."

Then he caught himself, as if he had said something he

hadn't meant to.

Christy remained silent, absorbing Todd's statement.

He called me by my Hawaiian name. He thinks I'd make a good missionary. Todd thinks we'd make great missionaries together! He wants to marry me! But if he goes on a surfing tour, when will I see him?

"Of course," Todd added quickly, "that's another bridge, isn't it? It has to be of your own choice."

"Right!" Christy joined in, camouflaging all her heart-pounding feelings. "Like your choice between college and surfing." She pointed toward the two lights on Molokai. "The closer you get to that decision, the clearer your choice will become."

"This sure has been an intense week," Todd said. "It seems like God had a lot He wanted to teach us."

Christy flashed back on Katie's prediction about God doing something in her life during this trip. *I wonder if this is what Katie meant by a God-thing?*

They were nearly back to shore now, and as the catamaran gracefully whisked its way into Lahaina Harbor, Christy delighted in the sight of the old whaling ship on display, ablaze with tiny white lights up one side all the way up its mast and down the other side. The Old Pioneer Inn, standing firmly before them, belched loud music and barrels of laughter from its open barroom doors.

Once again, Christy tried to imagine what Lahaina was like one hundred fifty years ago. She could picture the missionary ladies, sitting on their front lanai at the Baldwin house only a block away, fanning away the mosquitos in the warm summer-night air and praying for the sailors who had come into port that day.

That night Christy prayed for Paula. She prayed that night and every night until Paula left to go back to Wisconsin.

Things were different with Paula. Christy couldn't exactly say in what way, but ever since the trip to Hana, Paula had changed too. She hadn't become a Christian or even given any indication that she was interested. Still, she had mellowed in some way.

When Paula, Christy and her dad arrived at the airport the morning of Paula's flight back to Wisconsin, they found out the flight had been delayed nearly an hour. To Christy's amazement, Paula handled the news calmly.

This is the first time I've been in an airport with Paula when she hasn't drawn attention to us! Christy realized.

Paula's outfit may have drawn a bit of attention, though. She had on her Hana Road T-shirt; the shell bracelet Marti had bought her; some dangling, green gecko-lizard earrings; her hot pink sunglasses; and a fluorescent orange fanny pack she bought for herself that said "*Maui No Ka Oi.*" (Todd had explained it meant "Maui is the best.")

With an hour to wait, the two girls automatically drifted over to the huge windows and watched the planes taxi down the runway.

"It's been a full two weeks," Christy began.

"It sure has! I can't wait to get home and see if Alex wrote me yet. None of my friends are going to believe I met a guy from Denmark! I feel like I have something none of them do."

Christy felt like being snippy and saying, "Yeah, you still have your virginity, which is something none of them can ever get back."

Instead she said, "You have a lot that none of them have, Paula. And I don't just mean a boyfriend from Denmark."

"He's not my boyfriend, Christy. He's an international acquaintance." She sounded like she had practiced that a few times in front of the mirror while trying to come up with the perfect title for Alex. "He is cute, though, isn't he? He's so different from any of the guys at school—his accent and everything—and he was so nice to me. I still can't believe he called me the morning we left Maui."

"Guys *should* be nice to you, Paula. You're worthy of having the best guy in the whole world."

"You already have him," Paula said with a sincere but mischievous tone. "And you don't even appreciate him."

"Yes, I do!"

"No, you don't. He's the only boyfriend you've ever had, so you don't know how many creeps are out there. And he's so loyal to you, Christy! When I went surfing with him and when we went for pizza that one time, well, I don't think I should tell you this . . ."

"You'd better tell me!"

Paula adjusted her fanny pack, took off her sunglasses and said, "You're going to hate me, Christy, but I think you should hear this. When we went for pizza, I tried to, you know, come on to Todd and stuff. When we went surfing, he didn't act interested in me, and I figured it was because David was there."

Christy felt anger rising, but she kept it pushed down.

"So when we walked to the pizza place, he didn't respond or anything. Then he gave me this really sweet, big-brother talk about how girls shouldn't tease guys by coming on to them and by wearing, you know, skimpy clothes. How a girl shouldn't let a guy tease her by touching her too much or saying a bunch of flattering things."

Paula kept looking down. "He told me I should hold out for a hero. He made me feel I really deserved a prince and not just the first frog that came along. I want to find a guy who likes me for who I am and what I'm like on the inside, and not just for what he can get from me. I want to find a guy like Todd."

She looked up. "But don't worry! I'm not trying to take him away from you any more. He's totally in love with you, Christy. When you're around, no other girl exists. Believe me. I tried!"

Christy didn't know if she should be thrilled or furious.

"I wanted to tell you before I left," Paula said. "I guess it's a good thing the plane was late so I had a chance to."

"Yeah, a good thing," Christy said softly.

A smile crept back into Paula's expression. "I know, I know. Katie would tell me it's not a 'good thing' the plane is late—it's a 'God-thing.' "

"Does that mean you're beginning to agree with Katie about God-things?"

"I have to admit, Katie did make sense the other night at our slumber party when she said it was a God-thing Todd got stung and couldn't drive," Paula said.

"I don't know," Christy said. "That whole ordeal was pretty scary."

"Right, but like Katie said, look what happened. You had to drive the Hana Road, and as a result, when you took your driving test, you passed with flying colors! That never would've happened if Todd hadn't gotten stung."

"I don't know. I might have still passed my driving test, even if I hadn't driven in Maui."

"No, you wouldn't have. You would've been too scared. And you know what else? If I hadn't spent that time with Todd and if I hadn't seen the way he treats you and other girls, I wouldn't have gone back to setting high standards for myself. A lot of good things—oh, excuse me, a lot of God-things— happened on our trip, just like Katie said they would."

"Well, I'm still not positive I know exactly what a God-thing is, but I agree with you our trip was good for both of us."

Christy smiled, but inside she felt completely serious. "Paula, there's something else I wanted to talk to you about. I know we had some rough times during our trip, and I know I really came down hard on you. But I was trying to get you to become a Christian."

Paula squirmed a little bit, so Christy got right to the point. "I still want that for you really badly, but what I know now is that it has to be your decision. It's your bridge, like when Todd jumped and when I drove across in the Jeep. It has to be something you decide and commit to yourself, not something you get persuaded into. So, I promise to let up on all the stuff I've been writing you and trying to push on you. I'm still going to be praying for you, though."

"You can keep writing whatever you want. I don't mind. I like your letters. They're always really interesting. It's like I told you in Maui, you're probably right about God and everything. It's just that I'm the kind of person who has to figure things out for myself."

The two friends smiled their agreement, and then Christy started to cry tiny, salty tears. "I wish we could start this visit all over again and be as close at the beginning as we are to each other right now."

Paula let a tear or two drip. "But then we wouldn't have learned all the stuff we did."

Christy nodded and brushed her tears off her cheek. "I'm glad we keep trying, even though over the years our friendship kind of goes up and down."

"I'm glad we keep trying to rebuild it every time too," Paula agreed.

Christy pictured the church the missionaries built in Lahaina. Todd said the church was destroyed more than once. Then, the last time they built it, they learned from the past and faced the two doors so they could both open toward each other. That way, when the wild Kona winds came, they blew through the church rather than against it.

"I'm going to miss you, Paula," Christy said, picturing herself as one open door, facing another open door. She knew the strong winds of heaven now had freedom to blow through, rather than against, their friendship.

"I'm going to miss you too. I'll try to write more, I promise," Paula said. "And maybe I can come back out like at Christmas or Easter, because the way I see it, you still owe me a trip to Disneyland."

They both laughed. A few minutes later, when the plane boarded, the two friends said good-bye with laughter, hugs and tears.

It was a painful farewell for Christy, and she felt a sweet sadness all the way to Bob and Marti's house.

Bob was back from Maui, and he and Christy's dad had made plans to go car shopping after they took Paula to the airport. Marti met them at the door with a look that Christy had come to recognize. It said, "I know something you don't."

"Christy, dear," she said almost immediately, drawing her into the entryway. "You did bring a bathing suit with you, didn't you?"

"Yes."

"Splendid!" Marti clapped her hands together. "Then you don't need to go car shopping with the men; you can go lay out on the beach."

Christy knew something was up. She raced to the conclusion that Todd must have come back with Bob. He was probably out on the beach right now, where she first met him last summer. Marti was trying to set it up so Christy could be surprised when she went out on the beach and just "happened" to stumble into him.

Christy obediently scurried upstairs and slipped into her bathing suit. She pulled back the white eyelet curtains and checked out the beach to see if she could spot Todd's orange surfboard.

Nope. No sign of Todd or his board. She would play along with Marti's surprise and go on down to the beach.

The beach was crowded, as Christy would have expected for a Saturday afternoon in August. She wove her way around several different clumps of people, not sure who she should be looking for. Then someone called her name.

It was a girl's voice. She looked all around and didn't see anyone she recognized.

"Christy!" It came from a girl sitting all by herself on a beach towel near the water. Christy moved toward her, certain she had never seen the girl before.

She had blondish hair pulled back and wore a bikini that looked too tight for her pudgy stomach and thighs. The girl sat up straight and waved excitedly as Christy approached.

Who is she? How does she know me? I don't remember meeting anyone last summer who looks like her.

"Hello! You found me! Did your aunt keep it a surprise?"

As soon as she spoke, Christy recognized the unique accent. "Alissa?"

"Yes, hello! Did I surprise you?"

The girl-turned-young-woman, now stretched out on the beach towel, looked nothing like the tall, slim, blond-haired model who had slinked her way across the sand last summer.

Christy tossed down her towel and sat next to Alissa. "I can't believe it! How are you? What are you doing here? Where's your . . ." She was about to say "baby" but felt she was getting too personal.

"I mean, where are you staying?"

"So much has happened. I'm not surprised you didn't recognize me. No one ever told me how much having a baby

changes you both on the outside and the inside." Alissa
looked a bit shy, an expression Christy had never seen on
her before.

"My mom is doing so much better dealing with her
alcoholism that we decided to come back and finish the
vacation we never had last summer. We got here yesterday.
We're staying for three weeks. I couldn't wait to see you
and tell . . ." Alissa hesitated.

Christy was anxious to hear more, but she sat quietly,
using only her eyes to say "Go on."

"Last week I gave Shawna up for adoption."

"Alissa, you're kidding!"

"It was the hardest thing I've ever done. If it hadn't been
for you, I probably wouldn't have gone through with it."

"Me?" Christy felt startled. "What—I mean, why?"

"Didn't you get my letter?"

"No! Wait!" Christy tried to remember the message on
the mystery letter. Something about "I thought about what
you said . . ."

"Was it really short, and you didn't sign it?"

"Oh, did I forget to sign it? I had so much going on
during this last month. You see, I'd thought about giving up
Shawna for adoption a bunch of times, but everyone told me
I'd be sorry. I kept feeling so sure I should, because she
really needed a mommy *and* a daddy. And then I got your
letter, and I knew I had to do what *I* knew was right, even if
no one else agreed with me."

"What letter? What did I say?"

"It was right after you made cheerleader, and you decided

to give up your spot to the other girl because you knew it was the right thing to do. That took a lot of courage, Christy."

"Not really. At the time it didn't seem that hard, because Teri deserved to be cheerleader. Deep down, I knew that's what God wanted me to do."

"Exactly!" Alissa agreed enthusiastically. "I found out about this couple, through an adoption agency, who wanted a baby so much. The wife had had four or five miscarriages and several operations and still couldn't have a baby. I knew they would love Shawna and be the kind of parents she deserved.

"Oh, and Christy, you should've seen them when I signed the papers and handed her over to them. They took her in their arms, and the first thing they did was pray. Aloud! In front of the lawyers and everybody! They thanked God for answering their prayers and for giving them the baby they'd been asking for for so many years. Can you believe it?"

"Wow," Christy agreed, tears blurring her vision. "I can't believe it. Do you still feel like you did the right thing?"

"Oh yes, definitely. I gave them a long letter I wrote Shawna, along with a copy of a letter Todd wrote me all about Shawn. When she's old enough to understand, they promised to give her the letters. She'll know that when I gave her up it was because I wanted what was best for her. She'll know how much I loved her. I know I did the right thing."

A silence came between them. It was a silence filled with awe.

"There's something else, Christy," Alissa said, her round

face looking more like that of a little girl than that of the mother of an infant. "I don't know how to ask this."

"That's okay," Christy said, thinking nothing more could surprise her today. "Ask away. Anything."

"Okay. Well, I wanted to ask you how I could be like you and Todd. You know, the way you both are with God. I mean, I want God in my life and all those other things you and Todd both told me about in your letters. Only I don't know how to do it."

Christy felt her heart pounding wildly. "You mean you want to become a Christian?"

She couldn't believe that after two weeks of trying so hard to get Paula to turn her life over to the Lord, Alissa, of all people, had come to her.

"Yes, but I want to become a *real* Christian, like you and Todd and Frances, the lady at the Crisis Pregnancy Center. You guys all talk and act as if you know Jesus personally. That's what I want."

"Then tell Him that," Christy said excitedly. "Tell Him everything you're feeling. He already knows, but tell Him you're sorry for all the wrong stuff you've done and ask Him to forgive you. Then invite Him in and give Him everything in your life. He really loves you, Alissa. But then, you probably already know that." Christy paused to take a breath, not sure if she had said any of the right things.

"Yes, I do know God loves me, that He loves everybody. But do you think," Alissa hesitated. "Do you think God *wants* me?"

"Oh yes," Christy answered in a tight whisper. "Yes!"

A huge lump had nearly closed off her throat. "If only you knew how much He wants you!"

"Well, I know I want Him."

"Then tell Him," Christy said, swallowing back her rising emotions.

"Should I close my eyes?"

"I don't think it matters."

"I think I'll close them." Alissa closed her eyes, bowed her head and folded her hands, like a little girl in Sunday school.

Christy did the same, wondering only for a moment if any of the people around them might notice them praying. Then she decided it didn't matter. This was too much of a miracle to worry about what other people thought.

"Lord God, I don't really know what to say. You know how sorry I am for everything I've done in the past. I want to ask You to please forgive me. I don't want my life to be like that any more. I want You to come in and change me. I want You to take over my life. Amen."

Their eyes met before they had lifted their heads all the way. Christy broke into a huge smile.

Reaching over, she hugged Alissa and said, "I'm so excited for you! Todd is going to go totally wacko when he finds out! Did you know he's been praying for you for a whole year?"

Alissa blinked back a train of runaway tears and said lightheartedly, "Well, it worked! After I met you guys, I kept meeting more and more Christians. Things I couldn't explain started happening. I started to feel like there really was a God out there and that He wanted my attention."

"And what do you feel like now?" Christy asked.

"I feel like . . . like, I don't know. Like a little kid—all fresh and silly. I feel like running into the ocean, screaming and dancing all the way."

"Then come on!" Christy said, hopping up like an ignited spark. "Let's do it!"

"All right." Alissa giggled, springing to her feet.

"One, two, three, go!" Christy shouted.

With bare feet thumping into the sand, they ran together, waving their arms, shrieking and laughing like schoolgirls on the first day of summer.

Alissa brazenly shouted to the wind and the waves and any people who happened to be close enough to hear, "Jesus loves me!"

Then laughing wildly, impulsively, she shouted, "And I love Him!"

Exuberant and full of amazement at Alissa's transformation, Christy scooped her open hands and joyfully sent the spray shimmering through the air, showering Alissa with its sparkling mist. Alissa immediately sent a splash back at Christy, giggling like the giddy, trembling new creation she was.

Laughing until the tears came, Christy tilted her head back, squinted at the brilliant sun and said, "Now this, this is a God-thing!"